Autumncrow

AUTUMNCROW

Stories by
Cameron Chaney

*To my family, for encouraging my crazy imagination,
to Mrs. Clark, who gave me a voice,
to my YouTube creeps, for the undying support,
and to Jeff, who loves Halloween as much as I do.*

This is a work of fiction. All characters and events portrayed in this book are fictitious. Any resemblance to real people or events is purely coincidental.

Autumncrow Copyright © 2019 by Cameron Chaney
There Are Monsters Here Copyright © 2017
by Cameron Chaney

All rights reserved. No part of this book may be reproduced or transmitted in any form or by any means, including mechanical, electric, photocopying, or recording without prior written permission of the author.

*Cover art by Cameron Roubique
Exterior design by Christopher Rondina
Edited by J. David Osborne*

ISBN 9781688117341

Published by Library Macabre Press

Contents

Follow Me In..1

Pumpkin Light...6

Burnt Brownies..20

Frost..46

Saving Face...59

I Have No Mouth and I Must Feed...........................68

CRYP-TV..103

There Are Monsters Here...132

Follow Me In

My memory isn't as sharp as it used to be. For ages, it has been on a narrow decline, much like that rough hill you liked to roll down in the summer months, the one at the beach with stones instead of sand. Those are the days I remember the clearest. I think of little else now. Just you and me and that hill and the beach.

I recall always fretting that one of us would break our necks, but you'd click your tongue and push me over the edge. Soon, you'd be rolling along after me, laughing and whooping and hollering. Upon reaching the bottom of the dune, you said the same thing every time: "Was that not so bad, scaredy-cat?"

Though the creeping ache in my muscles said otherwise, it was impossible for me to disagree. You were radiant standing there, smiling and shaking the dirt from your hair and clothes. You were fearless, full of life and happiness and love. I couldn't look away.

You'd grab my hand and lead me up the shore. After

finding a spot with the nicest view, we would spread an old sheet over the pebbled ground and spend the rest of the afternoon there. It wasn't entirely comfortable, but you didn't seem to mind. You were forever distracted by the monsters in your notebooks. I watched as you scribbled away, filling page after page with the most unnerving tales I'd ever read. I never understood how someone as cheerful as you could dream up such ghastly stories. Or how someone as fearful as me could end up living with a horror novelist in Autumncrow Valley, "The Spookiest Town on Earth".

The beach was your favorite place to write. While Autumncrow bustled with the activities of a thousand tourists, the shoreline was silent and sacrosanct, vacant of sightseers, as if invisible to all other eyes. I pointed this out once, how odd it was that we were the only people to visit the beach. In response, you simply shrugged and said, "A realm of our own." This must be why you felt comfortable setting your pen to rest, pulling off your clothes, and running into the dark water, regardless of the chill in the air.

"Come, follow me in," you said. I wanted to protest out of fear that a tourist would choose this very moment for a stroll along the shore, but who was I kidding? I would follow you anywhere.

We swam and shivered and held each other close until the sun set in the overcast sky, then we returned home to our bed. You remember, the bed I always complained was too small. Now, years later, it is much too large.

I have tried to revisit the beach many times throughout the years, but I haven't been able to find it. The hill is still there at the edge of town, right where it has always been, but when I climb to the top and look down, all I see is Autumncrow Cemetery stretching on for hundreds of acres. Wherever you went after your final day, the cold waters of the lake followed, leaving behind an ocean of concrete and maple tree leaves.

I have spent countless hours standing at the top of that hill, trying to imagine the beach into existence. Maybe if I focused hard enough, it would come back to me. Maybe I would see you again, waving to me from the vast waters. Maybe I would join you.

Those images never materialized.

I don't climb that hill anymore, much like how I stopped visiting your grave when I realized you weren't really there. Besides, my knees aren't designed for that kind of impact these days. I prefer to recline in my chair with the television blaring. I lie there day and night, resting my eyes, but I don't sleep. I listen to the chatter of sitcom characters and think of you, of the waterfront, of those days when I was young and you were alive.

But somehow, impossibly, here you stand, staring at me from the entryway of our home. The streetlight drifts through the open front door, lighting your figure from behind. I stare at you and wonder if I have finally fallen asleep, but this doesn't feel like a dream. I rise from the chair and study your shape in the darkness of the living room. Static from the TV set illuminates your face just enough that I can see your smile and the twinkling of your kind eyes. You are as breathtaking as ever.

My body trembles as you draw nearer. You take my hand in yours and pull me toward the gaping doorway.

"Come," you whisper. "Follow me in."

We cross the threshold and enter Autumncrow's cool October night. We are moonlit travelers, navigating empty streets, waltzing through cornfields, and wandering the valley. All the while, the roaring of the vanishing beach grows louder and stronger. If the water had a voice, I believe it would sing my name; a lonely siren's call.

Together, we ascend the hill at the edge of town, the one we climbed countless times in our youth. My knees don't hold me back this time. The pain I carried in my joints, muscles, and heart for the past thirty years is no longer present. All I can feel is your warm hand in mine as we reach the top of the dune, reveling in the nostalgic sight. Our lake stretches before us, its surface igniting under the hand of the harvest moon. A breeze wafts across the water, carrying with it the aroma of algae and crisp Autumn harvest.

Tears trickle down my face, reflecting the cosmic glow of the moon and stars. You offer a soft smile before brushing the tears from my cheeks. Then you drop to your knees and pitch yourself over the edge of the dune. Joyful laughter fills the night as you roll toward the beach below, inviting me to do the same.

Home. I am finally home.

I don't hesitate. I forget all about my age and the possibility of injury, and I tumble along after you, feeling reckless and happy and free. We collide at the bottom, laughing so hard we can barely breathe. Neither of us move for a while. Shoulder to shoulder, we lie on our backs, staring at the stars overhead. They dance about in the sky like fireflies on a muggy summer night.

Finally, you stand and help me to my feet. "Was that not so bad, scaredy-cat?" The sound of your voice takes me off guard. It is deeper than before, much different than your normal husky tone.

Grasping my hand, you pull me toward the water, your smile widening with every step. Suddenly, I'm unsure if this is really you. Sometimes your eyes appear too dark; other times your teeth look too sharp. And the hands, tugging desperately at mine, are no longer human.

I should turn away, run back home and leave the looming beach behind, but who am I kidding? You are the author here, the narrator of my story. I will follow you anywhere.

We walk hand in hand toward the rippling black waters. And I follow you in.

Pumpkin Light

In my seventy-six years of living in Autumncrow Valley, there has never once been an imperfect Halloween. I have heard out-of-towners claim to have awoken on All Hallows' Eve to a ground covered in snow, or having had to run home after ten minutes of trick-or-treating because of a sudden downpour. A friend of mine who lives in Vermont once said that, as a young girl, she received a bruised eye due to a spontaneous hailstorm while she was out begging for candy. When she got home that night, her mother claimed it was God's punishment for participating in the Devil's holiday.

I, on the other hand, have never awoken to snow on Halloween. I have never been rained upon while trick-or-treating, and I've never been punched in the eye by God. This is because I have had the privilege of living here in Autumncrow. And I believe that, as you grow older, you too will share the same fortune as I. This is a strange town, yes, but it is a special place. We should feel blessed to live here.

Why don't you have another cookie, dear? Or a caramel apple. Please, make yourself comfortable. I know I have asked you here for your help, and I understand that you are eager to get back to your friends, but I must tell you a story first. It is very important that you know everything before we proceed.

Good, good. What a sweet girl you are. You remind me very much of myself at your age. In fact, I, too, dressed as a witch when I was eleven years old. It was Halloween of 1953 and I lived just down the road from where we are now, in the little blue house with the picket fence. Except the house was yellow when I was a girl, and it didn't have a garage. I remember waiting by my parents' station wagon, all dressed up in my witch's hat and black robe and striped purple stockings, ready to be driven the three miles to town.

You see, back in my day, this neighborhood wasn't like it is now. There weren't houses lined up as far as the eye can see. No, it was mostly corn fields, with more coyotes than there were homes. The walk to school in the morning was treacherous if the sun had yet to rise, creating a sense of danger that I enjoyed. This may be why my parents insisted on driving me into town instead of letting me walk.

This Halloween night, I stood in the driveway, gazing up at the sky—already filled with stars—and wondered why there seemed to be a full moon every Halloween. It was something I had never questioned before, something I was used to seeing. After all, it was Halloween; it should be a law for there to be a full moon on this sacred night. Realistically though, it just wasn't possible. As I got older, I started realizing just how odd Autumncrow seemed to be.

As I pondered all of this, some movement down the street caught my attention. There was a greenish light in the pumpkin patch behind Marie Cartwright's house. It was dim, but it's hard to miss even the faintest light when you're this deep in the countryside, surrounded by darkness.

I watched as the light rose in the air a few feet, bobbing in place, before coming to a pause. Squinting, I could make out the face of a simple jack-o'-lantern; round eyes, a triangular nose, a grinning mouth. It stayed there in the middle of the pumpkin patch, floating above the ground.

Me being the brave girl that I still am—and so very bored of waiting on my parents to get ready—I walked down the road toward Marie Cartwright's house.

Mrs. Cartwright was a peculiar woman. She didn't talk much to anyone, just stayed inside or tended to her garden. She often spent days on end in her kitchen, baking away until the sun set. Oh my, what wonderful scents floated from her open windows. I recall always wanting to go over and introduce myself, if only to sneak a taste of her delicious desserts. But I didn't, just because Marie didn't seem the friendliest of sorts. She could be a mean old witch for all I knew.

Her husband Gerald, on another note, was as sweet as could be. Very talkative. On warm days, he'd take a break from tending to his pumpkins and walk over just to say hi. He was always chomping on pumpkin seeds. Everyone in town would drive up in the weeks before Halloween to buy pumpkins from him. Gerald's Pumpkins, they were called. He had the best prices for miles around. Nowadays, Autumncrow is such a tourist trap that you're lucky to buy a pumpkin for less than five dollars.

Unfortunately, Gerald Cartwright passed away in the summer of 1953, just a few months prior to me seeing the jack-o'-lantern face in the field. He was seventy-five, just a year younger than I am now. It was very sad. People came from all over the valley to pay their respects, but Marie Cartwright refused to come out of her house. Everyone thought it was because she was a recluse, but I knew she was just very sad. From the way Gerald talked about her, it was clear that he loved his wife with all his soul, no matter how strange she may have been.

For the rest of the summer, I would look toward the pumpkin patch and try to find Gerald, hoping to see him working among the vines. Something told me he wasn't really gone, that he was still out there somewhere. And maybe he was in a sense, because while there was no funeral for Gerald, the kids at school said Marie had had her husband cremated, that she had scattered his ashes all over the pumpkin patch.

Of course, there were always those few naughty children who liked to fabricate stories to get the rest of us worked up. An example of one such story is that Marie murdered her husband and chopped his corpse into little pieces to use as baking ingredients. I laughed at such nonsense.

However, on this cool October night—walking toward the pumpkin patch and shivering in my witch costume—I felt the nerves take hold. Mr. Cartwright wouldn't have minded me being on his property, but as for Marie, I couldn't be sure. Maybe she really would chop me up and make me into a pie. Either way, this thought didn't stop me from entering the pumpkin patch and slowly approaching the grinning jack-o'-lantern.

I could see now that it was a white pumpkin, pure as day, not orange like the others in the patch. And it wasn't actually floating in the middle of the field as I had originally thought—it was being used as the head of a scarecrow. It peered down at me from its perch, its strange green light flickering in the night's breeze.

I recalled an early memory then, one of Mr. Cartwright telling me about white pumpkins, that they were white because they grew underground. *Ghost pumpkins*, he called them. I liked to think of them as fairy tale pumpkins.

This is a ghostly fairy tale scarecrow, I decided, though it was missing something very important—it had no arms. The sleeves of its orange and white plaid button-up hung limp with nothing stuffed inside to prop them upright.

This orange and white shirt, I realized, was the same shirt Mr. Cartwright used to wear every day when he was alive. Same for the overalls the scarecrow adorned, and the boots. I traced the fabric of the shirt with my fingertips, surprised to find that it was warm, as if a person was hiding inside. Glancing over my shoulder to make sure I wasn't being watched, I unfastened the top three buttons. A chilly breeze rustled the flannel, pushing the musty scent of dry rot up my nose. I suppressed a sneeze and peered beneath.

There was no human chest there, just thick, crisscrossing vines that moved right before my eyes, bursting through the ground and creeping up the torso of the scarecrow, slithering across its chest and traveling through the empty shirt sleeves, granting the scarecrow its very own set of arms. Long, delicate fingers stretched far and wide, protecting the pumpkins below from Halloween tricks.

I stood there, mouth agape, unable to comprehend what was happening. I took a step back, then another, and it was then that I saw what was really inside this being's pumpkin head. It wasn't a candle, but a large crystal ball. It glowed with that earthy green light, transforming the inside of the pumpkin into an otherworldly kaleidoscope. I wanted to reach inside and touch it, but a sudden voice made me spin on my heels.

"It's happening! Oh, it's really happening!"

Marie Cartwright stood behind me, her gray hair pinned up in a tight bun, much like my mother's hair on Sunday mornings. She wore an attractive black dress with purple lace accents that matched her eyeshadow. I'd never seen Mrs. Cartwright wear makeup before, nor did I imagine her the type to use perfume, but the sage-like fragrance emanating from her figure proved otherwise.

There was something else different about Marie Cartwright. Though she was beaming like a schoolgirl, the light from the crystal ball catching her tear-filled eyes, she looked frail, as if she had aged several years in the four months since her husband's passing. The makeup had been an attempt to cover what was still very clear: Mrs. Cartwright was ill.

The old woman looked at me and wiped away a tear. "Hello, my dear. I take it you're Macy? Gerald told me a lot about you. Please, come. I haven't much time, and I could use your help."

Marie offered her hand. On each outstretched finger, she wore beautiful rings of various sizes and styles. Most were darker shades of purple or burgundy, but one in particular glowed an eldritch green, identical to the light in the jack-o'-lantern. It pulsed before my eyes, a slow vibrant thrum of energy. I stared at that ring, hesitating. Then I took a few steps away from the woman.

I was never very good at speaking to strangers as a child. As Daddy always said, I was an odd duck, and he was right. It just took me a while to let my guard down, to let others in, especially in the company of an odd woman in the middle of a dark pumpkin patch.

"I can't. My—My mom and dad will be looking for me," I stuttered.

Marie looked over her shoulder toward my house. All was still in my driveway. The station wagon remained in its usual spot and my parents weren't yet standing on the front stoop, calling my name. Marie faced me and smiled the warmest of smiles. "They won't know you're gone, dear. It'll just take a few minutes. Trust me. You have nothing to be afraid of." She fluttered her fingers as if to assure me that I wasn't in any danger, then gave me a charming wink.

In that moment, I wanted to believe that every judgement I'd ever had about Mrs. Cartwright was completely unjustified, that I was a fool to think she was anything but a sweet woman who enjoyed keeping to herself... but still, that nagging feeling in my gut told me to be wary.

Reluctantly, I took Marie's hand and followed her across the pumpkin patch to the barn where Gerald used to keep his supplies. Entering the large open doors, I was greeted by the warm glow of candlelight and the smiling faces of dozens of jack-o'-lanterns scattered around, some sitting on bales of hay, others hanging from rafters, all giggling audibly if you listened close enough, like children at a sleepover trying to stay quiet. Or was that just the wind whistling through the rotting beams of the barn?

In the middle of the dirt floor, I saw a table littered with many strange objects; crystals, herbs, bubbling iron bowls, a tray of roasted pumpkin seeds, and—most notably—a very large, very old book.

Marie released my hand and hurried behind the table, popping a few pumpkin seeds into her mouth and flipping through pages of the musty tome.

"Here we are," she said, settling on a page. "Can you come here, dear? I could use your help reading from the book. It works better if there is more than one reciting the words."

"What's happening?" I didn't mean to say it, but the words escaped my mouth in a near whisper. The book, the candles, the crystals... what was all this stuff for? My hands were beginning to tremble.

Marie sighed. "I'm doing something very selfish, to be honest. But before he died, Gerald told me it was okay. That if it was something I needed to do, he was fine with it. And here we are."

Confused, I asked, "But... what do you mean?"

Marie wiped another tear from her cheek and smiled in a way that looked more like a frown. "Do you feel him?" she asked. "Here in the barn? In the field? Do you feel him like I do? He's all over, in each pumpkin, in every vine. In the air and earth. Sometimes I just stand out there in the pumpkin patch on cold nights... but I don't feel the cold, not one little bit. Because he's there, holding me from behind as we gaze up at the moon together." Mrs. Cartwright wrapped her arms around her shoulders, embracing herself, and closed her eyes. "My Gerald."

Now it sounded like the jack-o'-lanterns in the barn were weeping instead of giggling, soft moans of mourning.

A shiver crawled up my back. I pulled off my witch's hat

and held it close to my chest, as if it would protect me. "Mrs. Cartwright? Maybe we should go inside."

Marie opened her eyes and looked into mine. "Don't worry, love. I'll be alright. We're almost finished. I scattered Gerald's ashes over the pumpkin patch after he passed, and that seemed to do the trick. The soil here in Autumncrow... it's very dark. In more ways than one. But Gerald's ashes seemed to counterbalance that darkness. Light and dark came together and created a spark, just as I thought. That was the first step. Then I enchanted the crystal early this morning and—"

"Enchanted?" I interrupted.

"Yes, dear. Then I buried it along with a pumpkin seed in the field so it would capture Gerald's light."

"His... light?"

"His life, his light... All just words. After that, Gerald did the rest." Marie shifted her gaze out the open barn doors to the scarecrow standing in the pumpkin patch, its light twinkling in the night.

"What did Gerald do?" I asked, unable to hide the tremble in my voice. I was scared, yes, but there was a new feeling building a home in my throat, one that made me want to cry.

Marie kept her eyes on the scarecrow, as if it would flee into the night if she looked away. "Gerald grew from the ground. He became whole again, just for tonight. Just for me."

I bit my tongue. I didn't want to keep asking questions. I was beginning to sound like Lucy Dove from school, asking question after question as if she were five years old. But I had to know. I had to find out what was happening, why there was this feeling of intense sorrow pulling my heart into my stomach. So, I asked what would be my second to last question on this dark Halloween night: "Why?"

The dream-like daze on Marie's face melted away, erasing all hints of expression. Her eyes emptied, and she suddenly looked very tired. "I'm dying," she said. "Tonight is my last night; my last Halloween. I don't want to do it alone."

Marie finally pulled her gaze away from the pumpkin-headed man in the field and hung her head. Her shoulders shook, tears dripping onto the pages of her book.

This made me think of Daddy, how he cried the night his sister Margaret died of pneumonia. My mom had sat with him on the couch, holding him like she held me whenever I woke from a bad dream, cradling his head and smoothing his hair.

Before I knew what I was doing, I felt my mom's spirit deep inside me, pushing me across the barn to Mrs. Cartwright. I wrapped my arms around the old woman's trembling shoulders and held her close. She hugged me back, resting her head on my shoulder. We stood there together, sobbing as the jack-o'-lanterns observed. They were no longer smiling.

After a time, Marie pulled away and dabbed the water from her face with the hem of her dress. "Thank you, Macy," she said, sniffling. "What a sweet girl you are. You remind me very much of myself at your age..." She took a deep breath. "*Now.* We best finish the spell. As I said, two witches are better than one." She winked at me.

I grinned and returned my witch's hat to the place it was meant to be, over my dark brown hair.

"That's the Halloween spirit," Marie said. She threw another pumpkin seed in her mouth and pointed to the open page of her spell book. "This is something I wrote up earlier today. It's short but it'll help seal the deal. Take my hand?"

I did. We stood side by side and peered down at the simple hand-written words on the page. "Ready?" she asked.

Part of me feared what was to come, but I swallowed that feeling and nodded my head.

Marie took a deep calming breath and, together, we began reading:

"On this All Hallows' Eve,
when spirits play and the veil is thin,
come home, my Pumpkin Man.
Light my way and I'll follow you in."

With those words, the candlelight of each jack-o'-lantern flared so brightly, I had to shut my eyes. For a moment, I worried the barn had burst into flame, but the firelight soon returned to its usual mild glow, and I opened my eyes to see Marie Cartwright standing in the open doorway of the barn, staring out into the moonlit pumpkin patch.

I joined her in the doorway, watching as the scarecrow took its first steps across the field. Its movements were disjointed and clumsy, but instead of feeling fear at the sight of a living scarecrow lumbering toward me, I felt only amazement.

"It worked," Marie said. "He's almost here."

She began smoothing her hair into place and wiping the

tear streaks from her cheeks. I took a few steps back, thinking I should give them privacy but not wanting to look away.

The pumpkin man's fiery green light floated closer and closer. Soon, it was leaving the pumpkin patch in its wake and walking the final steps toward Marie. Its joints creaked and groaned. The wind rustled its clothes. Its light glowed brighter than ever.

Marie held out her arms to the scarecrow as it stumbled into the barn. "My Gerald," she whispered. "My brave husband. I asked a very difficult thing of you, I know. But still, you came."

I watched as the two embraced, Marie's head on the scarecrow's chest, the moon shining down on them, bathing them in blue. The two pulled away from each other. Marie looked up into the round, glowing eyeholes of the fairy tale pumpkin, and spoke. "It's time, my love."

The scarecrow stared at her. I wasn't sure what it was thinking—if it was thinking anything at all—but when it nodded its head in agreement, I knew that it knew.

Marie finally pulled her gaze away from the pumpkin man and gave me that same warm smile from before, one that made me feel like, had this not been her final night on earth, we might have become the best of friends. The old woman glanced toward her spell book for a moment, then looked back at me. She winked.

That simple gesture granted me more than I ever imagined, changing my path in life forever.

Hand in hand, Marie walked with her pumpkin man toward a bed of hay spread in the corner of the barn and laid down. The scarecrow crouched by her side, holding her close, stroking her hair. I watched as Mrs. Cartwright stared up in admiration at her husband, no trace of fear to be seen in her eyes. She now had a light to guide her way.

With a peaceful smile on her face, Marie Cartwright died.

A breeze whooshed through the open doorway of the barn and whisked out the candlelight of each jack-o'-lantern... all but one, that is. The pumpkin man, illuminating the darkness of the barn with its life light, stared down at Marie's body. It would have cried if it could.

No... not *it*. Him.

He was mourning her, I realized. Before he left to guide her onward, Gerald was taking a moment to say goodbye to his wife's body.

I stepped forward, breaking the silence with one last question. "Mr. Cartwright?"

The pumpkin man sat upright at the sound of my voice and—very slowly, neck creaking—he turned to face me. His light rested on me like a spotlight of hope in a storm.

He recognized me. He remembered.

The light of the crystal went out. Gerald Cartwright's new body slumped forward, and the scarecrow was just that; no more than vines and cloth. I was left standing alone in the darkness, taking in the sounds of the night. I left the barn knowing that I was walking away a different girl, not quite the same as I had been an hour ago.

When I returned home, it was as if no time had passed. My mother still sat at her makeup table, applying the last bit of blush to her cheeks and Dad was tying his shoes. "Ready to go?" he asked.

Neither of my parents noticed I was gone. I think I can

credit Marie for that.

After spending a fun night in Autumncrow Valley with my friends, trick-or-treating and going on enough rides at the Halloween Carnival to make my head spin, I returned to the Cartwright barn when I should have been snug in my bed. I gathered up Marie's book, her enchanted objects, the crystal ball from Gerald's pumpkin head, and I brought them home with me, knowing that the day would come when I, too, turned old and gray and would need a pumpkin man of my own to light my way.

I've been practicing a lot since that Halloween of 1953, and I know in my heart that my time has come, that this will be my last Halloween in this strange and magical town. I'll leave in happiness though, knowing that there is more magic waiting for me on the other side. And besides, there's somebody very special I'm excited to see again. It has been a long time, indeed.

All I need is a little help reading from my book here. After all, as Marie Cartwright once said, two witches are better than one. What do you say, dear?

BURNT BROWNIES

Bobby Tinkett stood at the bottom of the foyer staircase, his tiny gloved hand gripping the bannister—wrapped in leafy autumnal garland with various shades of red and orange—as if letting go would render him defenseless. The baby man stood in the center of the foyer, chowing down on a cauldron full of fun size chocolate bars and blocking the front door with his fat butt.

"Move!" Bobby Tinkett demanded.

The baby man looked up from his meal. "Huh?"

"I said move. I'm not screwing around!" Bobby pictured himself running at the baby man and pushing him out of the way, then thrusting open the door and taking off into the night. But the baby man, wearing nothing but a bonnet and an adult diaper, was enormous and smelled worse than a normal-sized baby. Bobby backed up a few steps, creating some distance between them, but he kept his eyes trained on the baby man, just in case he decided to kidnap him and feed him poisoned candy. Or whatever it is strangers do to seven-year-old boys on Halloween.

The baby man stared at Bobby for a moment, a look of

befuddlement on his porky face. Then he peeked into the living room. "Christine? Help."

Bobby's eyes widened. "Shh!" he said. "Do whatever you want to me, just don't tell my sister I'm here."

The baby man's left eyelid twitched. "Do... whatever I want to you? What are you even talking about?"

"Please don't tell Christine I'm down here," Bobby begged. "She'll murder me!" He looked around, making sure his sister wasn't on her way to address the situation. Bobby saw spiderwebs hanging in doorways, eyed the lighted silhouettes of ghosts being projected onto a nearby wall, spied an animatronic witch stirring her cauldron in a corner—but there was no sign of Christine.

Bobby sniffed the air. Buried beneath the sweat and fart stench of the baby man was the intoxicating aroma of freshly baked chocolate chip cookies drifting from the kitchen. His sister was probably in there now, preparing snacks for her stupid party.

"Sure, kid. Okay," the baby man said, shoving another candy bar into his mouth. "So, what are you supposed to be?"

Bobby knew he shouldn't speak to this stranger any more than he already had, but he couldn't pass an opportunity to talk about his costume. He had spent months piecing it together out of scraps he found lying around the house. Answering with pride, he said, "A zombie firefighter."

"Isn't that a little tasteless?" the baby man asked.

Bobby shrank back, as if he had just been slapped across the face. "Tasteless?"

"Yeah," the baby man said. "You know, insensitive to

firefighters. It seems pretty rude, bro."

"Rude? *Me?*" Bobby was breathless. How dare the baby man—who clearly had poor taste in costumes—criticize Bobby's outfit when he had put so much time and effort into making it?

"You're the one breaking into my house and eating all the candy that is s'pposed to be for trick-or-treaters," Bobby scolded.

The baby man looked down at the candy cauldron. "My bad. I thought this was for the party." He sat the cauldron down where he found it, on the floor next to the front door.

Feeling more confident, Bobby released his hold on the bannister and crossed his arms, adding, "And your costume is tasty to babies."

"Tasteless, not tasty," the baby man corrected. "And I didn't break in. I'm here for Christine's party. Shouldn't you be out trick-or-treating?"

A cloud of depression settled over Bobby Tinkett. He looked down at his red rubber boots. "Mom told Christine to take me trick-or-treating. But then Mom went to work, and Christine told me to go to bed..." Bobby felt a fiery rage overtake his sadness at the thought of his sister. "But I'm going trick-or-treating, no matter what that bitch says."

"This 'bitch' says you better get your skinny ass back up those stairs before I use you as lizard food." Christine, wearing her skintight 'Sexy Iguana' costume—as the Halloween store packaging had stated—sauntered into the foyer. She pointed a long, red-coated fingernail up the stairs. "Now."

Bobby was caught. He wanted to cry, but he held his ground instead, lifting his chin and balling his little hands into fists. "I'll call Mom. I'll tell her you won't take me trick-or-treating."

"I'll tell Mom you called me a bitch. Little boys who call their sisters bitches don't get to go trick-or-treating." She gave Bobby a poisonous grin, red lipstick smeared on her teeth.

"I'll tell Mom you're going to have a party," Bobby countered.

"Mom already knows, dipshit. She said I could throw a party as long as I don't have any alcohol. And as long as Macie Collings doesn't come."

The baby man turned to Christine. "What's wrong with Macie Collings?"

"She's dating that hot Italian guy who runs the haunted attraction on County Line Road. He's like 26. My mom doesn't approve."

"Let me go!" Bobby demanded. "Halloween comes once a year. After tonight is over, that's it. You never know, this could be my last Halloween. I could die tomorrow in a house fire. Or maybe next year, I'll be too grown up to go trick-or-treating." Bobby didn't think it was possible to be too old for trick-or-treating—that was almost the same as dying—but desperation gave him the will to say anything at the moment.

Christine rolled her eyes and strode across the foyer in three long steps. She leapt up the stairs like a panther going in for the kill and grabbed Bobby by the ear before his reflexes could catch up.

"I'm not going to let you ruin my party," Christine spat.

Bobby winced. Christine attempted to pull him up the stairs, but he resisted. "Please, Christine," he begged. "You took me out last year. We had fun. We always had fun. Why—?" He stopped.

"Why what?" Christine demanded. Her guests would be here in in twenty minutes; she didn't have time for this.

"Why do you hate me now?" Bobby asked. It was a question that had been on his mind since the beginning of the year, just after Christine's sixteenth birthday. Somewhere between then and now, his big sister had changed. She wasn't the same girl who used to watch monster movies with him every Friday night, the one who took him out for ice cream after school.

Christine eyed him, her face stoic and unreadable. Finally, she said, "I don't hate you. It's time for bed."

She dragged Bobby up the stairs by his ear. Though he struggled against his sister with everything he had, he knew his escape plan had failed. Halloween was ruined.

When Christine made her way back down the staircase, Mack Thompson, her boyfriend, was sitting on the bottom step, looking downright pitiful in his baby costume. Christine had begged him not to wear it, and he assured her countless times that he wouldn't. "You have my word, babe," he had said. As it turned out, Mack's word was as good as baby vomit. Surprise, surprise.

He held a platter of ghost-shaped cookies, the ones Christine had finished icing just before her brother's outburst. Mack had already eaten half of the cookies and was getting started on the rest.

"Why a zombie firefighter?" he asked, crumbs dropping from his mouth and sprinkling the uneaten cookies below.

"For God's sake, Mack, save some for the party," Christine said, grabbing the cookies away from him. She headed through the living room toward the kitchen, which was decked out in strands of purple and orange lighting. She sat the cookie tray on the kitchen island.

Mack followed and tried to find some free counter space to sit on, but every square inch was covered with bowls of chips, guacamole, cupcakes, finger sandwiches shaped like jack-o'-lanterns, and other snacks—so he opted to just eat until a spot opened up for him.

"You didn't answer my question," Mack said through a mouthful of brownies.

"What question?" Christine checked the clock. Ten minutes to go and the beer wasn't even here yet.

"Why is your bro dressed like a zombie firefighter?" Mack repeated. "That's a bit specific, don't you think?"

"I don't know. Bobby's a freak," Christine answered. "He's always telling me about this ghost that lives in our house—a man with burns all over his face. He even told me once that the burned man has a crush on me."

"Creepy," Mack said.

"I know. I'm constantly telling my mom that he needs a shrink, but she doesn't have time to deal with it. And the costume... that's just Bobby's way of scaring me. He knows I have a thing about fire."

"You do?"

Christine nodded.

"Why?" Mack asked.

"Just an old movie I saw as a kid." She opened the oven to check her second batch brownies. A black cloud wafted out, hitting Christine in the face. "Freaking damnit!" she screamed, immediately closing the door and turning off the oven. She waited, praying she hadn't released enough smoke to set off the detectors.

After twenty seconds of silence, she let out a relieved sigh.

"I think your brownies got burnt."

Christine glared at Mack. "No shit. I don't get it. They've only been in for like ten minutes."

"They're weak brownies anyway," Mack said, gesturing to the platter in his hands. "I've eaten at least ten of these things and I don't feel any different."

"They're not those kinds of brownies."

"Oh. Well, no one told me that." Mack looked around the kitchen. "Speaking of, I don't see any beer."

Christine rubbed her temples, trying to ward off an impending anxiety attack. "That's because there isn't any. Craig was supposed to be here thirty minutes ago with the kegs, but he's running late. Again."

Mack made a pouty face. "But I'm thirsty."

"There's pop on the table, you big baby," Christine told him.

"Not that kind of thirsty," Mack teased. His chocolatey frown curved upward in a grin. He pulled Christine to him, groping her waist before lowering his hands to her butt. He made to kiss her lips, but she pressed a hand against his face. "Gross! Your breath smells like my mom's store."

Christine's mother Jodie Tinkett—or Madame Tinkett, as she was known to locals and tourists alike—owned the gourmet candy shop in town. She was spending the rest of the night at Autumncrow's annual Halloween Carnival, handing out candy samples to visitors. In other words, she wouldn't know a thing about the party. Or the beer.

Mack snatched a decorative severed hand from the meat tray and placed it in front of his mouth. He belched, blew the stink against the open palm and sniffed. "You're right, my breath does smell like your mom's store. But I fail to see how that's a bad thing."

Christine resisted the urge to gag. Mack looked so pathetic standing there, half-naked in one of his grandpa's adult diapers, food all over his face. She was beginning to realize that no amount of popularity was worth the disaster that was Mack Thompson, whether he was quarterback of the Autumncrow Scarecrows or not. She couldn't wait to be rid of this oaf.

Tonight, she reminded herself. *It's all going to end tonight.*

"Your little brother seemed legit about calling your mom," Mack said as he continued his brownie binge. At this rate, he would probably eat the next batch too, leaving nothing for the guests. Christine took the platter from his hands and sat it on the other side of the kitchen island, far out of his reach. So, he started attacking the tortilla chips and guacamole instead.

Christine shook her head. "Bobby bought everything I said. He won't call her. And even if he does, 'Madame Tinkett' never carries her phone while she's working."

"What if he calls the store?" Mack asked.

"Then I'll make an excuse. Stop worrying, I have things under control." Christine smiled, confident the night was hers. Bobby be damned.

"Why do you hate me now?"

She had to admit, those words had caught her off guard. Her little brother had spoken them so quietly, as if afraid Christine would tell him exactly why she disliked him. But she didn't dislike him, not really. *Love* was a strong word, but she supposed she did love him in some way. Sure, she was hard on the kid, but he had gotten to be so damn annoying this past year, always whining and demanding attention.

Not to mention, the little creep spied on her almost daily at this point. She'd caught him hiding in her closet on numerous occasions. Sometimes, he would leap out of the shower to scare her while she was peeing, or she would come home from school to find that all her bedroom candles had been lit. She didn't know what this was supposed to mean, but now her fear of fire included pumpkin scented candles.

Simply put, Little Bobby Tinkett was a bit off. Naturally, her mother didn't agree with this viewpoint, but her mother wasn't around enough to see the signs. She was too busy running the shop, trying to pay the bills on her own now that her husband was out of the picture. No, Christine was the one who raised Bobby, not her mother. If it wasn't for Christine, Bobby wouldn't get his dinosaur shaped nuggets for dinner every evening, and that was the truth.

There was a loud knock at the front door, pulling Christine back into the present. Mack was staring at her.

"You okay?" he asked. "I was talking to you."

"I'm fine," Christine replied. "Go get the door. I need to figure out how to deal with these burnt brownies."

It was 9:30 PM, well past the allotted time for trick-or-treating, but that didn't stop Bobby from wearing his zombie firefighter costume until the fake blood on his face turned crusty.

Any other Halloween, he would have been at the carnival right now, stuffing his pillowcase to the brim with candy. He would be riding The Roller Ghoster repeatedly, screaming with every drop. He would be walking through Mayor Sherman's Haunted Courthouse attraction, trying to act afraid whenever a scarer in a bad rubber mask would jump out at him. Or he would be laughing at the silly lady who lived in the town-square oak tree. At least, Bobby assumed that's where the lady lived because she was always there. She wore an old, black dress that covered her dangling feet, and she had long, braided hair that was wrapped around one of the branches. Bobby always waved to her, hoping she would wave back, but she would just sway in the wind and make that same silly face at him, her eyes rolled back, tongue sticking out, cheeks all puffy. He wished he could go visit her now and have a fun night with his friends at the carnival, but he couldn't.

All because of Christine.

He thought of her now as he stared at his closed bedroom door, the sounds of her party booming through. He thought of Christine's stupid friends. He felt a burning sensation in his cheeks.

"Why don't you go show them who's boss?" a gruff, wheezing voice asked.

Bobby turned his head. He saw the burned man sitting next to him on the bed. The man came to Bobby's room every once in a while, but he usually preferred to visit Christine's room. He really liked her and would follow her everywhere: around the house, to school, to her boyfriend's house. Sometimes he'd just wait in her room, the surrounding candles igniting in his presence, lying on her bed until she got home. When she finally did, he'd watch while she completed her homework assignments or as she prepared dinner, trying to talk to her but getting no reply in return. That's because Christine couldn't see him. This frustrated the burned man, made him shout obscenities at her, words that Bobby never knew existed beforehand.

Out of fear that the man might hurt his sister, Bobby began to follow her as well, just to make sure she was safe. After all, the burned man acted a lot nicer whenever Bobby was around. Though he didn't seem very nice now.

His face was sizzling, skin bubbling and popping, sending yellowy liquid bursting onto Bobby's carpet and bedsheets. Bobby wasn't sure if his mother would be able to see the stains later, but Bobby would see them. He always would.

The burned man breathed heavily, his chest heaving up and down, his teeth bared behind partially non-existent lips. He had no eyelids, so his eyes were always wide and un-blinking, but now they were filled with a fire that hadn't been there before. It scared Bobby.

Turning his head, the burned man looked long and hard at the young boy, then grinned. "Do you love your sister?" he asked.

The temperature in the room began to rise, making

Bobby's costume stick to his skin. "Y—Yes," Bobby answered. "I guess."

"You guess?" the burned man wheezed.

Bobby nodded.

The man threw back his head and laughed, a nearly inaudible rasp, and stood from the bed, leaving behind a sticky, tar-like residue.

Melty skin, Bobby thought.

"You guess!" the man barked, clutching his stomach as if the laughter would make his guts fall out. As a matter of fact, Bobby could now see through a hole in the man's shirt that his guts *were* falling out. Charred intestines were threatening to spill onto Bobby's bedroom floor, and they would have, too, if the man hadn't been holding them inside.

Bobby wanted to close his eyes, but he couldn't look away.

The burned man stopped laughing and eyed the boy. All signs of humor evaporated. "How could you love someone like that?" he asked. "That bitch has ruined your whole Halloween. She's been a horrible sister to you all *year*."

"That's just because Mommy and Daddy aren't together any—" Bobby paused. The fire in the man's eyes burned into Bobby's. He could feel the heat on his face again.

Shaking his head, the burned man said, "That's no excuse. She has no right to treat you the way she does. I overheard her talking to that ugly boyfriend of hers, calling you a freak behind your back. How does that make you feel?"

Bobby frowned. "Bad," he said.

"I'll bet," the man said. He took a knee in front of

Bobby, keeping those flaming eyes locked on the boy's. "She is not a good sister, Bobby. She has treated you unfairly. She hates you. She wishes your dad took you with him, that way she wouldn't have to take care of you anymore. How does that make you feel...?"

Bobby looked deep into those wide eyes. They scared him a moment ago, but now... now they felt familiar to him, as if they were his own eyes.

"Are you—Are you a ghost?" Bobby asked.

The burned man slowly shook his head back and forth. *No.*

"Are you real?" Bobby said.

The burned man nodded.

"Why are you here?" Bobby pressed.

The man took Bobby's hands. They felt like charred hotdogs. The boy winced in pain. "Bobby. I'm here to help you help me. We need each other. Now answer my question: how does that make you feel?"

The burned man's fiery eyes were contagious.

"Mad," Bobby answered. "She makes me feel mad."

A wide, ghastly smile spread across the man's nearly nonexistent face. "Tell me, boy: do you like playing with fire?"

Mack Thompson dropped his red cup to the floor, beer splashing all over the carpet in the doorway of his girlfriend's bedroom. "What the hell, Christine?" he shouted.

Christine pulled away from Austin Deaver's lips, wiping

the smeared red lipstick from her mouth. "Huh?" she said. "Oh, Mack! Wow. This is awkward. We should really have a talk."

"A talk?" Mack exclaimed. His mouth hung wide, catching every fly in Autumncrow.

"Mack... I'm really sorry, man," Austin said, returning his vampire cape to its place around his neck. "I thought maybe you two weren't together anymore."

"We're not," Christine corrected.

"We're not?" Mack asked.

Christine faced Mack, squinting her eyes. "No. Sorry. It's over."

"Over?" Mack looked to the spilled beer at his feet, confused, as if wasting a perfectly good cup of beer was more perplexing to him than the situation at hand.

"That's what I said." Christine stood from the bed and strode into her bathroom, coming out with a roll of paper towels in hand. "Here you go."

She held the paper towels out to Mack. He stared at them.

"What?" he asked.

"Clean up your beer," she said.

Austin shifted awkwardly on the bed. "I should go," he said, standing and walking toward the door. "I'm going to get another drink."

"No," Christine ordered, motioning to the bed with the paper towel roll. "Sit down."

Austin paused in the middle of the room, looking from Christine to Mack, who still stood dumbfounded in the doorway. "Uh..."

"Sit," Christine repeated. Her voice was calm but firm,

confident in whatever idea was stirring in her head.

Austin obeyed, returning to his place on the mattress. Christine shoved the paper towels into Mack's hands. "Clean it up, 'kay?"

She strode over to Austin, straddling his lap and pressing her lips to his. He immediately pulled away, eyes wide. "Christine..."

She shushed him, placing a finger to his lips. Then she twisted her head to look back at Mack. He was a bulky silhouette standing in the doorway, framed by the light cast from the hallway, gripping the paper towel roll in one hand. A dry wheezing sound filled the room. It didn't sound like Mack, but then again Christine had never seen him get angry before, so this was a first.

Honestly, as crazy as it seemed, Christine wasn't sure if this whole scene would make Mack angry or not. She hoped it would, enough that he would finally get the picture. But every other time she had tried to break up with him, he'd laughed in her face and said he wasn't going anywhere, as if she had been pulling his chain. To her, something as extreme as making out with Austin Deaver was just another attempt at breaking the news. She knew it was cold, but she was fresh out of ideas. Best to just get it over and done with.

Fortunately, her plan worked.

A rage-fueled roar erupted from deep within Mack, making Christine's eyes widen in shock. The sound of the roar vibrated the bedframe against the wall. It shook the windows. It made the trick-or-treaters outside scream in surprise. It caused Austin Deaver to full-on piss his pants. And then silence.

"What the Sam Hill was that?" someone shouted downstairs.

Mack chucked the paper towels into the puddle of spilled beer and darted down the hall, taking the stairs two at a time. Christine heard the front door open before slamming shut.

Swallowing back the momentary terror of seeing Mack Thompson Hulk out, Christine forced a smile. "Thanks, Austin. You can go now." She climbed off his lap and let him stand.

"What was that all about?" he asked with a trembling voice, using his cape to obscure his piss-stained crotch. "Mack is gonna kill me."

"No. He won't." Christine crouched low to the ground and started mopping up the spilled beer. "Go enjoy the party. I'll be down soon."

Austin shook his head in disbelief as he exited the bedroom. "What is it with the girls in this town?" he muttered.

Christine sighed and sat on her heels, taking a moment to breathe as she watched Austin storm down the hall. *It's not just the girls, Austin dear,* said a foreign voice inside Christine. *It's all of us in this town. Everyone, everything. And that's the least of our worries.*

Christine massaged her temples. She had kept her cool through the whole scenario, but all the drama had drained her of energy and given her a pounding headache.

She knew this wasn't the end of it; there would be more migraine-inducing drama to come—the rumors, the side-eye glances in school hallways, the inevitable angry text messages and phone calls—but at least she was no longer tethered to Mack Thompson. Life could go back to the way it was before.

"Christine?"

She flinched and looked up at the figure standing over her in the doorway, scared at first that Mack had come back, scared that he would apologize and beg her to give him another chance. Scared that she would give in.

But it wasn't Mack. It was her little brother.

"Bobby," she said. "What are you doing up? You're supposed to be asleep."

"The burned man wants me to catch the house on fire and kill you."

Christine stared up at her brother for a beat, trying to comprehend what the hell she had just heard. This was a new one. Bobby had never outright threatened her life before.

Standing from her crouched position, Christine set her hands on Bobby's shoulders and stared into his eyes. "Listen. When the party is over, you can have all the brownies and cookies you want. But only if you go to bed. I'm sorry I didn't take you trick-or-treating, okay? But if you go and kill me because of it, I swear to God—"

Bobby shook his head. "No, *you* listen. I told him I couldn't do it, and he said I was a wimp. He said he'd find someone to make you burn, and that I would burn too. I'm not lying!"

Christine looked to the ceiling, baffled. She knew he wasn't lying; Bobby truly thought he was telling the truth.

"Well, why can't your ghost go and do it himself? Huh?"

"I don't think he can hurt anyone himself," Bobby murmured. "And he's not a ghost. He's something else."

"No, kid. *You're* something else." Christine started down the hall, ready to leave her crazy brother behind and get back to her party.

"Christine, please!" Bobby begged.

Before Christine reached the staircase, she stopped. She smelled something, a strong scent that drifted up the staircase and invaded the air around her. It reminded her of being at camp as a 12-year-old, of sitting around the campfire and telling ghost stories.

Screams began to ring out from downstairs. "The back door!" a boy screamed. "Go to the back door!"

Christine swirled on her heels and shot a glare at Bobby, one that was equal parts anger and terror. "What did you do?" she demanded.

"Nothing," Bobby said, backing away from her. "I told you, he tried to make me, but I couldn't do it. I was scared my Xbox would get all melty."

"What. Did. You. *Do*?" Panic landed heavily in Christine's stomach as the smell grew stronger.

"I told you, I didn't do anything! Stop looking at me like that!" Bobby shouted, covering his face with his hands.

Christine was no longer in control of her body. She spun around and stumbled down the stairs, choking on the thick grey smoke that lingered around her. When she reached the first-floor landing, she was greeted by the animatronic witch in the corner of the foyer, already engulfed in flames.

Christine thought of the melting wax figures in *House of Wax,* that old Vincent Price movie she had seen as a kid at the Screamplay Cinema in town. It was during one of their Halloween marathons, a theater filled with costumed children hyped up on candy. The other kids laughed at the scene, said the eyes melting out of the wax figures' heads looked funny, but it had scared Christine. It gave her nightmares involving a burning ballroom filled with dancing people. They were oblivious to the fact that they were being burned alive, unaware that their eyeballs were liquifying and trickling down their cheeks like milky tears. Night after night, they would smile and keep dancing until they were nothing but fleshy puddles on the floor. The nightmare finally stopped after a few months, but Christine never forgot their grinning faces, melting as the flames feasted on their bodies—Saturn devouring his children.

As frightening as the nightmares had been, the fiery landscape before Christine was worse. It was real. A sob fell from her throat as she watched the foyer of her childhood home—the one she had trudged through every day after school—become unrecognizable. Fire crawled up the walls and window drapes, licking the floor and ceiling.

The front door was already a gaping inferno. Christine could see through to the neighborhood outside, could see the people from surrounding homes gathering on the street, watching through tears as the Tinkett house—a home that had been standing since the early sixties—began to collapse in on itself. The fire was spreading at an alarming rate, pulling the house out from under it.

Where are the firefighters?!

Abandoning all hope of exiting through the front door, Christine shouted, "Bobby! Follow me!" over her shoulder and followed the screams of her friends sounding from the kitchen. She had to press tightly to the left-side wall of the living room to avoid being burned, but she quickly made it to the kitchen. Her friends were crowding out the back door, pushing and shoving as each tried to be the next one to reach safety.

Fortunately, while the kitchen was filled with smoke, the fire had yet to spread this far.

"Is this everyone?" Christine asked a boy at the back of the line. She remembered his face but didn't know his name.

"I guess. I don't know," he said, voice quivering. "I think so."

As soon as the boy spoke the words, Christine realized this wasn't true. Not everyone was here in the kitchen, trying to escape. There was still somebody inside the house, somebody she thought for sure had been behind her this whole time.

"Bobby!"

Christine turned and took off through the kitchen, her skin reddening as she neared the living room.

"Lit party, by the way!" the boy shouted after her.

When she reached the foyer, she was relieved to find the staircase untouched by the flames.

"Thank God," she whispered.

She ascended the stairs, praying Bobby was okay. She couldn't believe she had left him up here alone. She should have checked to make sure he was following. *Maybe,* Christine thought, *I am a bad sister after all.* No matter how weird the creep was, he was still her little brother. They had each been through a rough time since their father left, but instead of comforting Bobby, Christine had bailed on him too. She may have been taking care of him, but she definitely wasn't being his sister. Or his friend. He'd been trying so hard to get her attention all this time, and now look—he'd set the damn house on fire. She didn't know how, but that didn't matter. What mattered was getting out of here with Bobby in tow.

Crouching low to the ground to avoid inhaling smoke, Christine bounded down the second-floor hallway. Bobby was nowhere in sight, so he must have gone back to his bedroom. Christine would have to try not to smack him upside the head after she got them out of this.

She burst through Bobby's bedroom door to the sight of him sitting on the floor, unplugging the final Xbox cord from the back of his TV. "I got it!" he declared, holding up the console in both hands.

"I can't believe you!" Christine shouted, grabbing Bobby's wrist and yanking him to his feet. She went on and gave him a good thump to the back of the head anyway. She couldn't help it. "Let's go. Now."

She dragged Bobby to the staircase, the power cord of his Xbox trailing behind them.

"Wait!" Bobby pleaded. "I'm gonna drop my stuff!"

Christine ignored him. She started down the stairs, shielding her stinging eyes from the smoke. *Liquifying eyes. Melting eyes.* She choked and gagged but reminded herself that they were almost out. They were so close.

"Christine! I'm dropping—" Before Bobby could finish, one of his Xbox controllers tumbled from his hands and hit one step, then another, then another, and stopped on the exact step Christine had begun to take. Her foot landed squarely on the Xbox controller and, hand still locked with Bobby's, it was all air from there.

The world spun, a blurry Gravitron view of fire, stairs, ceiling, fire, stairs, ceiling, until Christine landed on the hardwood foyer floor with a crunching thud. Bobby came tumbling after.

Oh God, I'm dead I'm dead I'm dead, Christine thought. She opened her eyes, terrified that a blinding white light would linger before her, calling her name—that her life had been cut short because of her brother's Xbox controller, not even from the fire itself.

What a pitiful way to die...

But no, there wasn't a bright, shining light. There was only a view of the burning living room beyond the foyer, a room filled with dancing people—the men in traditional suits and bowties, the women in black, flowing dresses that became yellow as the frills whisked through flames. They danced around and around, smiling as they burned, as their eyes melted, as their flesh dripped to the floor, revealing the bone beneath.

Christine let out a weak whimper, quiet, but still loud enough to catch the attention of the dancers. They froze, turning their heads simultaneously as if it was part of their routine. Their empty eye sockets locked on the terrified girl before them. Then they started forward, stretching out their arms, reaching their skeletal fingers toward her, smiling with glee.

Knowing this was it, that the burning people had finally caught up to her, Christine pressed her hands to her eyes and screamed, screamed until she felt their fingers dig into her skin—

"Christine! Get up!"

Her eyes shot open. The people were gone. Bobby stood over her, his firefighter costume blackened with soot. He looked like a hero.

"Bobby..." Christine croaked. She pushed herself off the floor and wrapped her arms around her brother for the first time in months. He hesitated, still unwilling to let go of his Xbox. But it was busted from the fall anyway, so he dropped it and hugged his sister back, squeezing as tight as his little arms would allow.

They let go of each other. Christine placed her hands on his cheeks. "Are you hurt?"

"I'm okay," Bobby answered. "Are you?"

Christine sent a message through her body, trying to detect pain. It was remarkable, but she felt fine. "Yeah, I'm okay," she said.

She looked toward the front door. It was a charred, blackened hole, but the flames were gone. Through the ex-doorway, Christine and Bobby saw flashing lights and a watery mist—most likely from fire hoses—showering down on the house and front lawn. She could hear shouting coming from deep within the home, implying that the firefighters had already made their way inside before the two of them had tumbled down the stairs. Instead of getting the attention of the firefighters, Christine snatched Bobby's hand and led him out of the house onto the wet, blackened grass.

A tear rolled down her cheek. They'd made it. They were alive.

The neighbors remained on the street, observing the scene from a safe distance. Some would later report that the house occasionally took on the appearance of a flaming jack-o'-lantern, grinning down at them with a mouthful of sharply carved teeth. The face would flicker away, only to return a few minutes later if you happened to be watching closely enough. It would become a legend that the townsfolk would share with their children and grandchildren for generations to come.

Christine and Bobby stumbled past paramedics and firefighters, all of them running about in urgency, treating those who had received minor injuries in the blaze but not stopping to help either of the Tinkett children.

"Help... Help..." Christine heard herself say, but they were too busy to hear.

Christine scanned the crowd. *Mom*, she thought. *Mom has to be here somewhere.*

Finally, she spotted her mother, still in her orange Madame Tinkett's Sweets apron, her face painted like a skeleton. She was screaming at a police officer, begging the woman to let her pass, that her children were still inside, damnit!

"MOM!" Christine yelled. "We're here!"

She tugged on Bobby's arm, trying to pull him toward their mother, but he refused. "Wait, Christine. Look."

He pointed across the yard to a cop car sitting in the middle of the grass, its lights swirling. A face stared out the back window, a big shirtless guy with a bonnet in his short blond hair.

"Mack," Christine whimpered.

He stared hard into the flames, a tired but somewhat arrogant grin on his face. And Christine knew.

"Oh, no," she whimpered. "Oh, no no..."

"The burned man made *him* do it instead," Bobby said.

Christine didn't hear him. Or, rather, she did hear him but she was so used to Bobby's talk of the burned man that it just didn't register.

"Let's go to Mom," she said, her eyes still locked on her ex-boyfriend. "We need to tell her we're okay."

"We're not okay," Bobby said.

Christine turned to her brother. "What did you say?"

"We're not okay," he repeated. "We're ghosts."

Christine was crying again. "Please, Bobby," she said, wiping a tear from her cheek. "Don't say that."

"But it's true. We died in there," he said, looking toward the house. "They're pulling us out right now."

"Oh Jesus, *NO!*" a woman's voice screeched, causing a chill to creep up Christine's back despite the heat of the dying fire.

Her mother broke past the officer and raced across the yard, ran straight toward the mouth of the house. "My babies!" she screamed. "Not my babies!"

Christine's eyes followed her mother until she reached the front porch of the house. A firefighter grabbed the hysterical woman before she could get any closer.

Walking down the porch steps were two firefighters, each carrying the motionless body of a child; one held a strawberry blonde teenage girl dressed in her 'Sexy Iguana' costume and the other cradled an 8-year-old boy, looking very much like a fallen firefighter.

"The girl's neck is broken," one firefighter told another. "The boy has no pulse."

Their mother landed on her knees, reaching for her children, begging for this to be a dream, or maybe one of her son's Halloween pranks. But it wasn't. Bobby wasn't going to say, "Gotcha," nor would their mother wake up in a cold sweat.

Neither would Christine.

Christine held a hand to her mouth, tears streaming down her face. They hadn't made it. They weren't alive.

She remembered the dancing people she had seen in the living room, the ones from her nightmares all those years ago. She wondered if they were still in the house. Or maybe they were outside with her right now, dancing among the surrounding neighbors, laughing.

She clung tightly to Bobby's hand, wishing she had done so more often in life, wishing she had protected him, much like she had when they were younger.

She would make sure they never strayed apart ever again.

"Christine?" a voice spoke from behind the Tinkett children. It was a deep voice, one that crackled like burning autumn leaves. It was a voice Bobby knew all too well, but it was new to Christine; she had been much too alive to hear it before.

That was a different story now.

Christine didn't want to turn around, didn't want to see the burned face that would be staring back at her. But she knew she would have to look into those lidless eyes soon enough.

"Can you hear me, Christine?" the voice wheezed. "Can you see me now?"

Frost

When I was sixteen years old, I ran away from home. I'd made the decision to run away two years prior but decided I wouldn't get very far without a license and a car, so I waited until I had both. That alone was a challenge. Most of the students at my Colorado Springs high school received brand new cars for their fifteenth birthdays, primed and ready for the countless hours of driver's ed to come. Not me.

On the morning of my sixteenth birthday, I stepped outside, ready to begin my trek to school with buttered toast in hand, when I saw the tan 1991 Pontiac 6000 parked in the driveway. The windshield was cracked, the headlights were busted, and the fender sagged at both ends, frowning. It looked like it was in pain.

Dad appeared at my side, shoving the keys against my chest. "Go on, Ollie. Take it for a spin," he said. He took the toast from my hand and crunched into it.

Being the obedient son that I was—and too afraid to argue—I did as my father wished and stepped toward the rust bucket. The ghosts of a million cigarettes manifested themselves as the driver's side door creaked open. I held my breath and sat on the nicotine stained seat, receiving a stab in the ass from a loose spring poking through the fabric. I winced and repositioned my butt so that the point jutted between my thighs, then I turned the key in the ignition.

Nothing happened. I tried again and again, wondering what I was doing wrong. My dad opened the door and propped an elbow against the roof of the car, casting a shadow over me. "It don't run," he said.

I stared at him, unsure how to respond. My brain often went fuzzy in this man's presence, leaving me confused and tongue-tied.

He took another bite of the toast, chewing slowly, as if I didn't have anywhere to be. Swallowing, he said, "If you want somethin', you gotta do it yourself. Gives you experience. You can use the garage. I got the tools for the job. Good luck."

Dad patted the hood of the car and walked toward his beautiful home, probably to count the money he had stashed away in one of his safes. Oh, he had money, and plenty of it. But it was *his* money, just like this was *his* house. Mom and I were nothing but squatters in his mind.

I sat there for a moment or two, staring at the grimy dashboard as my soul sunk beneath my body. I knew nothing about cars, but I would have to learn if I was ever going to get out of here.

I spent the following week watching countless YouTube videos on car repair and reading automotive books from the library, trying to make sense of everything under the hood. I quickly discovered that the Pontiac 6000 worked. My dad had just disconnected a bunch of things before giving it to me. You know, to give me experience. The car still looked like shit and sounded like a generator on the brink of exploding, but at least it would take me away from here.

By the time early October rolled around, I was ready to go. My bags were packed and I had two hundred dollars left over from my summer job at the bowling alley. Enough to get me by for a while, I naively thought.

I didn't bother to leave a note. At best, my parents would skim over it the next morning and shrug. Mom wouldn't be surprised, and Dad wouldn't care. One less mouth to feed, and all that. No, a note would be a waste of time. My open bedroom window would say enough.

It was cloudy that night. No moon, no stars. I could barely see as I crept around the house toward the driveway. Everything I needed was already tucked inside the trunk of my car. All I had to do was climb in and drive away, so that's exactly what I did.

As crazy as it sounds, I didn't know what I would do or where I would go. Even if I had made a plan beforehand, it's not like I owned a cell phone or GPS to show me the way—Dad didn't allow them in his house, said the government used electronic devices to listen in on us. So, I just drove, letting the road guide me how it saw fit.

Morning became afternoon, afternoon became night. Besides stopping for gas, I stuck to the road, too nervous to eat and too afraid to stay in any one place for too long. Though I doubted my parents cared I was gone, I couldn't help but imagine my dad tracking me down and dragging me back home, maybe giving me a bruised eye again, or worse.

Those thoughts made me drive faster.

Driving at night is a much different experience than driving during the day. I'd briefly experienced this while driving with a permit, but someone had been in the car with me at the time, and I hadn't been running low on sleep. Now, I felt like I was cruising through a dream. The yellow lines on the road a few feet ahead were all that existed. Everything else was blackness. No lights, no cars, no buildings or houses, no way of knowing where I was.

I drove onward for miles, eyes heavy and corroded with sleep. I needed to stop, to find someplace to pull over and rest, but there was nothing in sight. While I couldn't afford a motel, I didn't want to just pull over on the side of this eerie road. I had to find a rest stop or parking lot. Even an old barn would do, a place to squat until morning came, when I was able to gage my surroundings.

As if in answer to my wishes, my headlights illuminated a structure up ahead. A smile spread across my face for the first time in a while. Maybe I was getting closer to civilization. Maybe I'd find a place to sleep. As I eased on the brakes, creeping up to the tiny building, my hopes were dashed.

It was a lonely covered bridge with a stone base and wooden walls the color of crabapples. The black roof was newly placed, white trim freshly painted. It may have been picturesque in daylight, but it had the exact opposite effect now.

"Come on in," it seemed to say as it swallowed the road in one mighty gulp. *"I won't bite."*

The darkness inside the maw of this inanimate beast was thicker than the darkness outside it. I had imaginings of a large purple tongue flopping about inside under the cover of blackness, wanting nothing more than to wrap around a teenage runaway and pull him into its empty belly.

To the right side of the bridge was a plaque that read:

Welcome to Autumncrow Valley, Ohio,
the Spookiest Town on Earth!

Ohio, huh? The last sign I remembered seeing was one welcoming me to Alabama. That had been hours ago, but I didn't see how it was possible to make it from Alabama to a small Ohio town in such a short amount of time.

I eyed the sign, gripping the steering wheel with trembling hands, and peered deep into the Cimmerian gloom of the covered bridge. I turned the car around.

There was no way in hell I was driving over that bridge. I didn't even want to know what was on the other side. Instead, I would go the opposite direction until I hit an intersection, then I'd turn another way. The thing was, I couldn't remember how I came about this ghostly road in the first place. It was as if I'd fallen asleep on the interstate and awoken here. But that wasn't possible... was it?

I sped through the night, leaving the covered bridge in my wake, eager to see city lights in the distance signifying safety.

Those lights never materialized.

A large object appeared in the middle of the road, no more than three-hundred feet ahead. Shouting obscenities, I slammed on the breaks, screeching to a halt at the mouth of a covered bridge. I sat there for several seconds, staring in disbelief at the sign beside the entrance, a sign welcoming me to Autumncrow, Ohio.

"This can't be," I whispered.

I had been driving straight for miles now. There had been no turns in the road, no twists or bends, no way of circling back to this point.

And yet, here you are, the bridge seemed to say.

I scrubbed sleep from my eyes, aggravated and tired and filled with fatigue. Just the act of keeping my eyes open was becoming unbearable. I needed to sleep, to become unconscious of this nightmare I was trapped in.

So, I did the only thing I knew to do—I let off the break and sped through the covered bridge.

I don't know what I was expecting. To drive forever in the tenebrosity of the bridge? To be swallowed whole, plunging down, down into a hellish wonderland?

Neither of those things happened. Instead, I coasted right through, welcomed on the other side by a bright halfmoon that bathed the autumn leaves above in silvery light. Holding the surrounding woods at bay were sturdy wooden fences running parallel to the inclining road, each painted a deep dark red, the same color as the bridge behind me.

Upward I drove, following the steep hill clear to the top. Here, a whole other world opened up before me, a stark contrast to the dark wasteland I'd encountered on the other side of the bridge. It was a world made of cobblestone sidewalks, of redbrick houses and Tudor mansions, of gravestones and apple trees, of leaf-strewn roads that wound down valley hills, of cornfields and black cats and glow-in-the-dark paper skeletons.

Driving through the dark, empty streets of this sleepy

little town—this "Autumncrow Valley"—I felt a sense of safety that postponed my drowsiness for the time being. My parents, if they decided to look for me, would never find me here. No one would. I felt shielded, as if suddenly invisible to the rest of the world.

Or maybe I was too tired to think straight.

Yawning, I pulled into the parking lot of a tiny playground bordering a stretch of forest not far from Main Street. Shutting off my car, the sound of the motor was replaced by chirping crickets and the high-pitched croak of a treefrog in the distance.

Rummaging in my backpack, I found a box of Ritz crackers that I scarcely remembered swiping from the kitchen before leaving. I devoured an entire sleeve with half a jar of peanut butter before leaning back in my seat, letting the cool air wash over me.

It had been a long day, to say the least. The car seat was far from comfortable, but I was so tired I could have slept in a dumpster. In no time, my thoughts and worries drifted away, carried off into morning like dead leaves on an autumn breeze.

That's when a knock awakened me.

I shot upright, squinting against dawn's morning glow as I looked in the direction of the noise: my driver's side window. The temperature must have dipped below freezing while I was asleep because a thick layer of frost covered all the windows of my car, blocking my view of the visitor.

The knock came again, a light *tap-tap-tap* on the glass with the hint of shadow cast by a set of knuckles.

Hands shaking, I double-checked the locks on all four doors, not knowing if there was a police officer outside my car or someone who meant harm. Either option would spell deep trouble. My heart raced as I gathered the nerve to speak. "Who's—" My voice broke off, so I cleared the phlegm from my throat and tried again. "Who's there?"

There was a long stretch of silence. I sat, waiting as worry and dread consumed me, praying that I hadn't been caught, that it wasn't my dad out there right now trying to lure me out of the car so he could beat me within an inch of my life—

"Hi," the soft voice of a man said.

That was it. Just *"Hi."*

"Who's there?" I repeated, relieved to hear that the voice sounded nothing like my father's.

"Nobody," the man said. "John."

I waited for the man to say more, but he didn't. "John who?" I pressed, the feeling of uneasiness returning to my gut.

"Just John," he said. The tone of his voice was a sad whisper, barely audible through the glass. It sounded as if he had been crying.

A cold shiver licked my spine as I opened the storage console to my right. I found a McDonald's napkin and, reluctantly, I pressed it to the window, attempting to clear the glass. It didn't do a bit of good; the window was frosted on the outside.

To be honest, this came as a relief. I didn't want to see the quiet man standing outside my car. In fact, my mind was screaming at me to drive away right then, to put my car into gear and go go *go*. But I couldn't do that. The defrost would take a good fifteen minutes to clear the windshield. Until then, I wouldn't be able to see enough to drive anywhere.

"What's your name?" the voice asked.

I didn't answer, just felt my throat tighten as my stomach twisted in on itself. Upon leaving Colorado Springs, I thought I was going to take control of my life, to escape from the horrors at home and the loneliness I faced at school, to become someone different. Now I was just a sixteen-year-old kid again, one who wished his mother had reminded him to bring a jacket to fight the cold, one who wished his father was there to tell the man outside to step away from the damn car.

"Where are you going?" the man asked. "Are you leaving home?"

"Why would you say that?" I demanded, maybe a little too quickly. Christ, I wished I could stop shaking.

"Your license plate says Colorado," the man replied gently.

"I'm visiting. I'm just vis—iting." My voice knotted in my throat. *Awful, terrible, no good liar.*

Silence. It stretched on and on.

Screw it, I thought. I turned the key in the ignition and started the car, flipping on the defrost.

"I've frightened you," the man finally said. "I'm sorry."

I prayed the windshield would clear quickly so I could leave. I wanted to get out of here, to hit the road and leave this strange man behind.

"What's your name?" the man pressed.

"Tom," I lied, hoping it would satisfy him.

There was a light chuckle outside, but it was void of humor. It could have easily been a sob. "Tom," the man echoed. "I was like you once, Tom. I left home early. I didn't have a plan. Just wanted out. I wound up here. Never left."

Okay, so this guy was a hobo. I had never spoken to a homeless person before, had only seen them standing on street corners, holding signs begging for help. "Heroin," my dad would tell me when I was a little kid. "They want money for heroin. Never give them your hard-earned cash, Ollie. You just keep walking." Though the signs normally asked for a job, not money, I heeded my dad's warnings. I'd look the other way. Better to give them nothing than to enable them. I'm sure that's what most people think in those situations. The question was, what did this man want? Money for drugs? A ride?

The lower part of the windshield was beginning to thaw, though it still had a long way to go. I flicked on the wipers in hopes that they would clear the ice faster, but they were still frozen in place.

"You're not ready to be in this world alone. It's a scary place," the homeless man said.

I could make out the man's inky silhouette through the frost now that the day was growing brighter. He was leaning close to the window, swaying from side to side like a metronome.

He's trying to see through the glass, I realized. *He's trying to see me.*

Very slowly, the man began to circle my car, his silhouette gliding over the windows like a small passing cloud. "A scary place..." he continued, the melancholy tremble returning to his voice. "This *town* is a scary place. It isn't what it seems. Go home. You can make it another two years until college, I know you can. Give yourself a chance.

Go home, Ollie..."

I stopped breathing. I may have even stopped existing in those few seconds after the quiet man spoke my name. *Ollie... Ollie... Go home, Ollie...*

The sound of my name on the man's lips brought a frightful tear to my eye. I couldn't remember what fake name I had given him a moment ago, but I knew for a fact I hadn't told him my real name.

After a few seconds of shocked silence, I finally managed to say, "How do you know my name?"

The man's silhouette paused at the passenger side window, silent for two, five, ten seconds. Then he finally spoke.

"I'll be seeing you."

The man's shadow disappeared from the window as the crunching of gravel signaled his departure. I was left shivering in the stranger's absence, running those ominous words over and over in my head: *"I'll be seeing you..."*

Five minutes later, the windshield cleared. I was sitting in a rest stop parking lot just off the highway. The tiny park I had pulled into last night, with its swing sets and teetertotters and monkey bars, was gone.

I hopped out of my Pontiac and found a map tucked into a kiosk inside the rest stop. Maps were foreign language to me but from what I could gather, I was in Santa Rosa, Florida, more than thirteen hours south of Autumncrow Valley, Ohio. I had never been to the town. It just wasn't possible.

Except I *had* been there. And it wasn't some dream. I remembered it all so crisply; the rolling valleys peppered with red and orange trees, the small shop windows adorned with vintage Halloween masks and jack-o'-lanterns, the manicured lawns of charming neighborhood homes... the voice of the stranger outside my car.

I spent the rest of the day on the highway. Even though I told myself I wasn't going anywhere near that tiny town and the man's ominous message—*"I'll be seeing you..."*—I kept driving toward it anyway. It was as if something was calling me there, a voice in the back of my mind whispering, *"Follow me in."*

In thirteen hours, just as dusk was beginning to blanket the surrounding cornfields in darkness, I drove over a covered bridge, past a brightly painted wooden sign welcoming me to Autumncrow Valley.

That was almost ten years ago. I haven't left Autumncrow since.

The locals aren't so bad. After my car broke down, they started giving me a lift here and there, but the town is small enough that I rarely need to bother anyone. That pretty lady Jodie Tinkett who runs the gourmet candy store on Main Street is the kindest to me of anyone. Whenever she sees me walking past, she runs out and hands me a buckeye or a block of pumpkin fudge. The poor woman lost both her children in a housefire a couple years ago, but still strives to brighten some homeless man's day with something sweet.

The tourists are a different tale altogether. I see the way they look at me, or the way they *don't* look at me, rather. I can hear what they're thinking, and it's exactly what my daddy would have thought; *"Heroin... wants money for drugs... hard-earned cash... don't give..."*

I don't sleep at night. It is hard to do that in this town. There are too many strange noises, too many voices. And the shadows... they never stop moving. I hide in different places every night, but the things in the shadows always have a way of finding me. Nightfall is a time for running, crying, praying, wishing for a way out of this cursed place, for a way to undo what's already been done.

One more chance. I need one more chance.

That is why, on this chilly morning as the sun begins to rise and the monsters retreat into hiding for yet another day, I feel hopeful. Maybe, just maybe, my second chance has finally arrived.

I slip from my hiding place—a tiny concrete tunnel at the edge of the park—and step toward the parking lot, toward the tan Pontiac 6000 with its Colorado license plates and frowning fender. My heart races. My bottom lip trembles. Tears trickle down my stubbly cheeks.

As I draw nearer, I am reminded of that night on the dark country road, of ending up at the covered bridge again even after driving in the opposite direction. I could have sped back and forth forever and ever, but I would have ended up in the same place every time, just as I am now.

I raise a shaking weathered fist to the frosted driver's side window, and I knock.

Saving Face

Moby Mudd was not happy to call the restroom building his home, but that's exactly what it was, whether he liked it or not.

Home sweet home, he thought as he wiggled a shopping cart through the restroom door. *Home sweet friggin' home...*

He'd borrowed the cart from the local Super-Duper Mart a couple of years ago, and since then, it had become his best friend. He'd even started talking to it, named it Angelica after his late wife.

"Alright, Angelica. What do we have today?" Moby said, picking over the shopping cart's contents. He quickly realized that there wasn't much to get excited about. He'd loaded up on some brush for tonight's fire, as well as a few discarded department store catalogues that would serve as kindling. Then there was the football Moby had taken into custody when one of the teenagers he'd been spying on threw the ball a little too hard.

Moby Mudd had been watching the group from the trees all afternoon, completely out of sight, waiting for the inevitable moment when the ball would come sailing over the fence into the forest. When it did, Moby made a dive for it, hoping one of the seven boys would have the guts to hop the rusty fence and come searching.

"C'mere..." Moby had whispered, cradling the ball to his chest as if it were a newborn infant. "C'mere..."

Instead, Moby'd issued an aggravated scoff when the boys wandered away from the park, accepting the loss of their football. Like most kids in the town of Autumncrow, they knew the forest was off limits. After all, people went missing in there. Others turned up dead. It was a dangerous place.

They were right. Moby could attest to that.

Months ago, on that cold rainy night, Moby had only wanted to take shelter inside the park's abandoned restroom. This, of course, hadn't been his first choice. He had tried to duck inside the tiny concrete tunnel located in the playground just outside the forest, but that young homeless buck—his name was Ollie-something—had already made a home inside, murmuring in his sleep about spooks and shadow creatures.

Crazy bastard, Moby had thought. There'd been a time when Moby was the only vagrant in Autumncrow, but more had started turning up in recent years, presenting tougher panhandling competition and fewer warm places to seek out.

Seeing the restroom building just a few yards inside the forest, Moby decided to give it a shot. He was damn cold, and he didn't really believe in all that nonsense about the woods anyway—at least, not at the time. Besides, he couldn't possibly get lost when the building could be seen from the tree line. So, Moby found a hole in the fence separating the woods from the park and, pushing his stolen shopping cart through the gap, entered the forest.

Moby Mudd never came out.

The trees took what little freedom he'd had, ripped away his identity, poisoned his mind, made it impossible for him to ever leave again. Well... not impossible. He could leave. The trees reminded him of that every night as he drifted to sleep, offering their words of wisdom in ghostly whispers.

"Moby..." they said. *"Moby, dear? You can leave. You can get out and live a better life than you ever had before. You just need to find someone new. Someone new. Someone new..."*

At first, Moby didn't know what this meant, but it soon began to make sense. He just had to lure someone inside the forest. Someone new to take his place.

And so, Moby Mudd returned to the forest's edge every morning, attempting to bait someone—anyone—who happened to pass through the park. Unfortunately, people aren't as stupid as they are in horror films. When someone hears a mysterious voice floating from the woods, inviting them inside, they don't grab their magnifying glass and head in to investigate. They get the hell outta there. *Wimps...* Maybe today would be different.

Under the cover of foliage and brush, Moby watched as a little boy and his father tossed a softball back and forth. The man shouted not-so-constructive criticism at his boy, like:

"Don't throw it like that, Jimmy. Throw it like this!"

"You're bending your wrist too much!"

"You're not bending your wrist enough!"

"You're not going to get anywhere in life if you can't do something as simple as throwing a ball!"

The kid, no more than ten years old, looked as if he were about to cry. "Can we go home now? We've been going all morning. Mom said lunch would be ready at 11:30 and that was an hour ago. I'm hungry."

The father made pig-like snorting sounds at his son. The boy hung his head in shame.

Moby hadn't been watching for very long, but he already despised this man. This prick didn't realize what a good life he was living. He had a home to go back to, a wife who was working hard to get lunch ready for her family, and he had a son—a beautiful kid made of his own flesh and blood. Moby would have done anything to have a life like that, to have a place to sleep, to have his sweet Angelica back in his arms. To be a father again.

"Stop being an oinker and throw the damn ball!" the man roared at his boy.

Jimmy lifted his head, his face no longer puckered in sadness but in anger. He brought his arm upward and hurled the ball at his father. It sailed past the man's head, narrowly missing him, and plunged into the woods. Moby Mudd scrambled after it, scooping the ball up and holding it as if it was worth a million bucks. Then he waited.

"Come on in, asshole," Moby whispered. "Come get your boy's ball."

Instead, the man shouted, "You trying to kill me, kid? What do you think you're doing, huh?" He ran at his son and slapped him across the face. Jimmy's hand flew to his cheek, but he didn't cry. Even from his spot in the trees,

Moby could see the embarrassed look in the kid's eyes. This wasn't the first time his father had hit him.

Fire churned in Moby's gut.

"Now you listen to me." The man pointed a finger in his son's face. "You go in there and retrieve that ball. You hear me, fatso?"

Jimmy's hand dropped from his cheek. He stared at his father in shock. "But—But I..." he stuttered. "I can't! Those woods are haunted. Everyone at school says so."

"Stop being a girl, Jimmy," his father scolded through clinched teeth. "Go get the damn ball."

"But... It's okay," the boy pleaded. "Really. I don't want to play anymore anyway. I'm tired."

The man grabbed Jimmy's face in his hands, squeezing his cheeks together, as if he could crush the kid's head between his palms if he really wanted to. "Go. Get. The ball."

Abusive piece of shit, Moby thought. The poor kid was obviously terrified. Even if the forest wasn't haunted—and it most certainly was—there was still the risk of poison ivy or injury. Didn't this guy know that people have died in here? Gone missing...? Moby had only been a father for two short years thanks to the night of the accident, but he could do a much better job than this clown.

Defeated, the boy walked to the forest's edge, staring hesitantly into the trees. Moby felt bad for the kid, but he knew there was only one way to lure that sorry excuse for a father inside. So, Moby peeked out from behind a tree and whispered, "Hey, Jimmy... I got your ball."

Just as planned, the kid took one look at Moby Mudd and unleashed a scream of pure terror. He took off running toward his father, whimpering and pointing to the trees. "A man... a man..."

"What the hell are you going on about?" Jimmy's father demanded.

"A SCARY MAN!" Jimmy cried. "He... he—"

Another sharp slap. Jimmy stopped crying, but the terror stayed put. Moby had given the kid quite a scare.

"Now. Did this man take your ball?"

"He..." Jimmy whimpered, trying to stay calm. "He said he had it. But it's okay. He can keep it. Let's go home. Please?"

"No. When someone takes something that isn't his, you gotta take it back. You gotta fight for what's yours, Jimmy. You hear me? You gotta *fight!*" The man rolled up his sleeves. "You stay put and watch how it's done." With that, the man lumbered toward the trees.

"No, Daddy, no!" the boy yelled.

"Yes, Daddy, yes," Moby Mudd whispered.

The man ignored his son, climbed the fence, and shouted, "Alright creep, where you at? You think you can just steal things from little kids?"

The man shuffled through the underbrush. He acted tough but he was a fairly skinny guy, about the same size as Moby.

How convenient, Moby thought. *How very, very perfect...*

He crouched low so as not to be seen. "C'mere, Daddy," he muttered. "Come and get the ball. I'm not gonna hurtcha' too bad."

The man stumbled aimlessly, the branches of the trees reaching for his face. As soon as he pushed one limb out of the way, another took its place, scratching at his cheeks, poking his eyes, making him growl in rage.

"Ow! Asshole tree! I'll show you!"

He grabbed at a vine that seemed to wrap itself around his head, as if it were a starving snake. He wrenched at it, tugging, twisting, pulling, until it finally cracked in half, freeing his field of vision. He expected to see yet another branch coming toward his face, but instead he was met with a very different sight.

Not two inches from his nose was the face of Moby Mudd. Or rather, where his face had once been. As if nibbled away by a murder of crows, the skin of Moby's face was gone, revealing nothing but a bloody, grinning skull. Random chunks of maggot-infested flesh clung to the bone. Gooey eyeballs rested inside his sockets, staring the man down in desperate hunger.

"Want to play ball?" Moby spoke.

The man froze, his eyes widening in shock, mouth gaping as if prepared to issue a blood-curdling scream. But before he could, Moby wheezed in excitement and jammed his dirty fingers into the man's open mouth, latching onto his lips and the insides of his cheeks. The man gagged as one of Moby's dirty fingers jammed against his throat. Moby repositioned his fingers, latching even tighter onto the man's lips, and began to pull.

Jimmy's father groaned in confusion and pain as his legs gave out, sending him to his knees. Unable to move, he stared up into the murderous eyes of Moby Mudd.

Moby braced a foot against the man's chest, giving him more leverage to pull and pull and pull and...

"I'm really sorry about this," Moby apologized. "But the trees said this is the only way. Someone has to take my place, and why not a vile scumbag like you, eh?"

With these words, the man let loose a garbled, heart-stopping scream as the skin under his jaw split and pulled loose with a sickening *SHLOOP!* Moby Mudd flew backward, falling onto his back, a shower of red raining upon him.

The man—his head now nothing but a bloody skull—collapsed onto the forest floor, unmoving.

Moby sat up, looking down at what he now held in his hands: his ticket out of the woods. The man's skin looked like a Halloween mask, so Moby treated it as such, slipping his skull through the neck-hole and pulling it down, down. The skin mask slid on smoothly, making wet squishy sounds as he readjusted the eyeholes until he could see through them. He could already feel the skin shaping to his skull, molding to the bone. It was becoming part of him and he a part of it.

Nice fit.

With a newly restored identity, Moby Mudd waltzed toward the man's body. The asshole wasn't dead. In time he would wake up and, like Moby, would find himself unable to leave the dark forest. Unless he, too, lured some poor unfortunate soul inside to be his substitute. In that case, Moby could have a problem down the road as the man might come to reclaim his own face. But until then, Moby felt perfectly comfortable walking around in this man's shoes. And his skin.

Moby slipped into the man's clothes and practically skipped out of the forest.

"Are you okay?" Jimmy exclaimed, running to greet who he believed to be his father. "I heard you scream! Is that blood on your shirt?"

Looking at his new son, Moby felt those warm fatherly feelings of yesteryear flutter inside his chest. He smiled at Jimmy and said, "I'm okay, buddy. Really. Hey, look what I found!" He held out the softball.

Jimmy looked at the ball, then at Moby, then at the forest. "Did you see... the skeleton man?"

"Sure did," Moby said. "I wrestled this ball right out of his hands. I said, 'That'll teach you to steal from my boy!' You shoulda' seen the look on his face!"

I HAVE NO MOUTH
AND I MUST FEED

1

Ellen Reid was on spiderweb duty.

She pulled the sticky strands of cotton apart, as wide as her wingspan would allow, and began sticking them to every available surface. Luca would say she was going crazy with the webs again—that clean-up would be a 'bitch'—but he couldn't pretend the spiderwebs didn't enhance the atmosphere. In Ellen's opinion, they tied everything together, covering imperfections in the décor, hiding flaws that would otherwise distract from the experience. Luca could critique her choices all he wanted, but he knew she was right. It was obvious in the way he stood, arms crossed, all his weight on one foot as he tapped the toes of the other, surveying the setup like a picky film director before saying, "Just not so many webs, okay?"

Yeah, he knew Ellen had the best web-manship in all of Autumncrow. He was just too proud to admit it. Why else would he leave her in charge of spiderwebbing every day?

Now if only she could convince him to let her use glow-in-the-dark webs instead...

Ellen finished decorating the "Vampire Lounge"—as Luca had coined it—and stood back, surveying her work. Not only did the set appear to be straight out of a classic Hammer horror film, but the Nosferatu-esque vampire dummies were extremely convincing. Luca was an artist, this much was true. Each vampire snoozed in open coffins that leaned upright against the stone walls. In the middle of the room sat a marble slab, one that would soon be the resting place of the vampire queen. As guests walked by, the queen would awaken from her slumber and snatch at them, hissing and baring her fangs.

Such cheese, Ellen thought.

In the eight years since Luca's haunted attraction first opened for business, Ellen had begged him relentlessly to let her be the vampire queen. After all, she was curvy enough to fill that off-brand Elvira costume. *And* she had the acting skills to pull off something far more convincing than the standard tongue flicking and teeth clicking. She didn't take four years of theater at Autumncrow University for nothing.

But no, Luca Holbrook had to have it his way. Every year, he gave the job to whomever he was currently dating. Last year, it was that skinny blonde bitch Hellen Cox. This year, it was that other skinny blonde bitch Macy Collings.

Ellen desperately wanted to slap some sense into Luca, inform him that black girls such as herself could just as easily be vampire queens. She had watched the 2002 film *Queen of the Damned,* starring the late Aaliyah as the queen herself, enough times to be sure of this. But Luca had a type and he was going to stick with it.

Sighing, Ellen inspected the Vampire Lounge one last time. Maybe it could use another package of spiderwebs after all. At *least* one more. She grabbed a fresh bag and ripped it open when she heard the voice of Alvin Bright speak from behind, breaking her concentration.

"What do you think?"

She turned, expecting to see Alvin with some new prop he had rigged up, possibly another animatronic zombie that puked green slime into a rusty barrel. Alvin had a thing for those. Instead, Ellen was met with the pale, lifeless face of a mannequin. It wore a blonde wig, bob-style, and a gray turtleneck sweater with yellow and pink stripes. Its lips were painted a glossy red, its cheeks a soft pink. It was straight out of Ellen's nightmares.

"Get that thing away from me!" Ellen shouted. She darted across the room and jumped on top of the vampire queen's stone slab, looking down at Alvin and his creepy new friend.

Alvin laughed maniacally, his beer belly bouncing before him like the gut of a sadistic Santa Claus. "That was great!" he exclaimed, using a lock of the mannequin's wig to wipe tears of joy from his eyes. "I hope everyone who walks through the haunt will react the same way."

"I don't want that thing anywhere near me," Ellen said. "Seriously, Alvin. I can handle just about anything, but that? I hate it. It looks like the mannequin from that YouTube video."

Chuckling, Alvin said, "That's because it *is* the mannequin from that YouTube video." He pulled out his phone and punched in his passcode.

"What are you doing?" Ellen demanded.

Alvin ignored her and hit a button. Right on cue, the mannequin's head swiveled to the left, blue eyes locking on Ellen. Its mouth began to move, issuing words sung in a garbled, mechanical voice. *"I feel fantastic... Hey hey heeeey..."*

"Hell *no!*" Ellen screamed. "Luca! *Luca!* Get in here, please! Alvin is being a dick again!"

The mannequin continued its little song while Alvin clutched his gut, laughing hysterically. "Wow," he said between gasps for air. "Luca said she would creep you out, but I did not expect you to react like this."

Luca bounded into the Vampire Lounge, Macy Collings at his heels. "What's going on?" he asked. He spotted Ellen standing on top of the vampire queen's resting place and crossed his arms, shaking his head. "Ellie. I appreciate your passion, but I already told you. Macy is the vampire queen this year." Luca motioned to his girlfriend who stood in the doorway, a smug grin stretching her plump lips. "If this is some kind of audition, I—"

"Shut the hell up, Luca. This isn't about your vampire princess," Ellen said, pointing at Macy, whose cocky expression dissolved into a dissatisfied glare.

"That's *queen* to you, bitch," Macy retorted.

Ellen gritted her teeth as a cauldron bubbled in her chest. She had harbored an intense resentment toward Macy for several months now, ever since the girl first donned the vampire queen dress and wormed her way into Ellen's close-knit Dungeon of Death family, but the two had made it this far without any direct confrontations. Oh, there had been verbal jabs here and there, accompanied by annoyed glares and rude hand gestures when the other wasn't looking, but this was the first time Ellen considered punching Macy Collings in her perfect face. She would have, too, had that stupid mannequin not been in the room, daring Ellen to come nearer.

"Hey, enough," Luca demanded. "We don't need any drama this close to opening day." He turned to Ellen and said, "What's this all abou—?" Luca paused, finally noticing the mannequin in Alvin's arms. He nodded, his mouth curving upward at the edges. "I see."

"It's not funny," Ellen said.

"I'm not laughing," Luca said, though he was clearly fighting the urge.

"You should've seen her reaction, man," Alvin told Luca. "One look at Tara and *bang!* She jumped up there and hasn't come down since. She's been up there for *hours.*"

Ellen scoffed. "A minute. I've been up here for a minute."

"*Hours*," Alvin fibbed. "At least that long."

Having endured enough of their mockery, Ellen forced herself off the edge of the vampire queen's slab, ignoring the nervous tremble of her legs. She eyed the mannequin, praying its song would come to an end, but it was likely that Alvin had it on an endless loop.

"Please leave... Run run run run..."

Ellen shivered.

Tara. That's what Alvin had called the thing, the same name as the mannequin from the viral video Ellen hated so much. It took a lot to scare Ellen—she had grown up in Autumncrow after all, which was literally patented "The

Spookiest Town on Earth"—but something about the lo-fi quality of that video and the theories surrounding its origin gave her the creeps.

Macy Collings stepped away from Luca and circled Alvin and his mannequin, as if sizing the two of them up. Seeing Macy and Tara side-by-side, it was easy to notice several similarities between the two. The haircut, the slender frame, the sharp cheekbones. The only difference was that Macy wouldn't be caught dead in a sweater that ugly.

"Hmm..." Macy said, tapping a finger to her chin. "I like her. *Great* thigh gap. I don't see what's so scary."

"Well, she is your own kind," Ellen muttered.

Macy turned to Ellen and narrowed her eyes. "I don't see why you have to be so mean. What's your deal?"

Ellen glanced at the ceiling and pointed a finger toward the mannequin. "That's my deal. I want it out of here." She directed her attention at Luca. "Please make Alvin get rid of it," she pleaded. "I won't be able to work here knowing it's in the building with me."

"Relax, Ellie," Alvin said before Luca could reply. "I worked really hard to make this thing look exactly like Tara from the video. Here..." He brought out his phone again and pressed a button. Tara's unnerving song ended.

"Better?" Alvin asked.

"I still don't like it," Ellen said.

Macy rolled her eyes. "Well, I know I'm just the vampire princess and my opinion probably doesn't matter, but I think you're overreacting."

"You're right, your opinion doesn't matter," Ellen shot.

"Oh, my God!" Macy stomped her foot like a five-year-old being denied a cell phone. "Does anyone else see how mean she's being? What the actual frick?"

"Agreed," Luca said. "Knock it off, Ellen. Macy didn't do anything to you."

"Yeah. What's your deal, dude?" Alvin scolded.

Ellen opened and closed her mouth, unable to utter a reply. Luca and Alvin had never ganged up on her like this before. Ever since they were teenagers marathoning horror movies in Luca's basement, the guys had always had her back, sticking up for her whenever she needed an army. Now they stared at Ellen with disapproval, making her feel small and unwanted.

Sure, Ellen was being hard on Macy, but she had heard enough of this girl's snide remarks to last her the rest of October. Halloween was Ellen's favorite holiday. She didn't want it ruined by some spoiled bimbo who sat around whining when she'd already gotten everything she wanted.

Ellen was a veteran of Dungeon of Death. She had been here since the beginning, ever since that stormy summer night when Luca had his epiphany to build a haunted house. The three of them were just kids, seniors in high school with no idea where they would end up. They had come a long way since then, working tirelessly to make Dungeon of Death as scary as it could be. Ellen had been a part of this legacy for ten years, and she loved it, but she wasn't going to be disrespected any longer. Swallowing the bitter taste of rejection, Ellen stiffened her spine and held her chin high.

Luca stared at Ellen for a moment and, realizing she was on the verge of quitting, issued a long sigh. If Ellen quit, the haunt would be set back an entire week, at least. Luca couldn't afford that. Rubbing the back of his neck, he glanced at Alvin. "I'm sorry, man. I know how hard you worked on it, but—"

"I'm not dumping Tara," Alvin said. "C'mon, dude, the whole idea is to scare people. If Ellie thinks Tara is scary, then I did my job. It's hard to scare Ellie." He looked at Ellen, eyebrows curved upward, lips pouting. It was his sad puppy-dog face, a strategy he used against Ellen whenever he was desperate to win her affection, and it rarely failed. Sighing, Ellen closed her eyes. As much as she wanted to stand her ground, she couldn't resist her friend's adorable face.

"It's fine, forget it," she said. "Tara can stay. I can handle her."

"Hell yeah, you can!" Alvin exclaimed. He turned his attention to Tara. "You hear that, babe? You and I are gonna be spending a lot more time together."

The mannequin's lifeless eyes stayed locked on Ellen. There was a slight smile on its rubber face, noticeable to no one except Ellen. Had it been smiling before?

"Why did you name her Tara anyway?" Macy asked Alvin. "Ex-girlfriend?"

"What? No," Alvin replied. "Tara the Android. You know, from the video."

"Oh, yeah," Macy said, laughing awkwardly, cheeks reddening. "Right, right..."

What a poser, Ellen thought.

Apparently, Luca realized this too because he stepped up behind Macy, put his lips to her ear, and explained in a deep, eerie voice, "It's from this strange video online. People say a serial killer built a robot just like this one.

Dressed it in the clothes of one of his victims. He named it Tara and programmed it to sing that song as a way to symbolize what he wished his victims would say instead of screaming for help. He wanted the girls he kidnapped to 'feel fantastic' about being in his company." Luca mimed air quotes on either side of Macy's head, his fingertips brushing her cheeks.

Macy closed her eyes, shivering. "I love it when you do that low, spooky voice, baby," she whispered.

Ellen blanched and shared a look with Alvin who grinned like a schoolboy watching an R-rated movie from behind his parents' couch. Between the creepy mannequin and the bizarre flirtations unfolding before her, Ellen wanted to go home to her cats more than ever.

Luca continued, his lips touching Macy's ear now. "The killer filmed clips of Tara singing her song in various awkward poses, edited the clips together, and posted it online. At one point in the video, the murderer points his camera at a spot in his backyard, zooming in very slowly. It's been said that this is the spot where he buried his victims. Just before eating their bodies."

Macy opened her eyes, staring at Tara the Android with fascination. "Wow," she whispered.

"Bullshit," Alvin interjected, breaking the mood. "The killer didn't eat the bodies. How could he bury his victims in the backyard if he already ate them?"

Luca shot a disdainful glare at his friend. "That's because you can't eat bones, dumbass. He needed a place to bury the bones. *Bones!*"

Alvin shook his head. "Don't listen to him, Macy. I've read all kinds of stories about Tara the Android, but I've never read anything about the killer eating his victims. He's making it up."

"For the love of God, guys! It's all made up," Ellen corrected. "There was never a killer. Apparently, some weirdo built Tara as a kind of music project. He posted a bunch of videos of her on his website hoping she'd become famous and he'd make a bunch of money. That's it."

"She's right," Alvin said. "The goal was for Tara to be the world's first android music star. As for that creepy shot of the backyard, it could have been edited in by someone else whenever they uploaded it to YouTube. Just to make it seem like a murderer made the video."

"Well, that's boring. I like the serial killer story more," Macy said. She narrowed her eyes at Ellen and grinned. "If you know so much about the video, why are you still afraid of it? I thought you weren't afraid of *anything*."

"Everyone's afraid of something," Ellen said, eying the mannequin. It stared back with that same lifeless smile. At least, Ellen hoped it was lifeless.

2

Weeks later, Ellen stepped out of The Little Bookshoppe of Curiosities, careful not to step in a puddle on the sidewalk. She tugged on the hood of her yellow raincoat, shielding her hair from the light, misting rain that had overtaken Autumncrow that day.

Main Street was dead, a rare sight this time of year. The muggy, damp night had scared off every tourist, sending them back to their bed and breakfasts. Ellen actually enjoyed the weather, thought it gave the town an extra spooky touch.

Ellen's coworker Willow exited the bookstore, switching off the lights and flipping the OPEN sign to CLOSED. "It's freezing out here," she complained.

"Are you kidding? It's so humid," Ellen said, marveling at the damp landscape looming before her. Wrought iron lampposts were placed every few yards along Main Street, their soft glow simply cosmetic, designed only to caress the fog instead of emanating any significant light. The moon—waxing on the eve of a full moon Halloween—did all the work, casting long, eerie shadows over the cobblestone streets. The town itself was ghostlike, as if it had died sometime between the year it was founded and the present day. But instead of going to the grave, Autumncrow continued onward, always growing, unaware of its demise. At least, that's how Ellen thought of it.

She'd had this idea since she was a young girl. It all started on the night of the sleepover. A girl in her class had extended the invitation to Ellen, said it would be a night filled with pizza and scary movies. It had been a fun time, but that all changed when Ellen awoke in the middle of the night. The moment her eyelids sprung open, she'd thought: *This house... Something is in this house...*

Some unknown presence had passed through the home, entered the bedroom she and her friends were sleeping in. Ellen could feel it watching them, a nightmarish visitor hovering in the air above, waiting for one of the girls to wake up and scream, scream for Mommy to please, please come!

Yeessssss... Call for Mommy... Call for Mommy, you little shit! She won't see me, but I see you. I... see... you...

Ellen had to get out.

Her friends dozed on as she packed her things, careful not to glance away from her quickly moving hands. She had been terrified of what she would see if she looked up. Perhaps something evil sitting on the ceiling, or red eyes watching from a corner.

Having stuffed her belongings in her backpack, Ellen made a dash for the front door, anticipating the feeling of safety she would encounter outside. That feeling never came. Making her way home through the quiet, sleeping town, she realized she was in even more danger than she had been a moment ago. Voices whispered her name from the alleyways. Deep growls rumbled in the sewers. And then there was the distinct, consistent hammering noise, one that echoed through the night like the beating of an iron heart.

Autumncrow is growing, Ellen had thought, remembering the stories of houses appearing where they had never been before, of streets shifting locations overnight or disappearing completely. She had never seen these things for herself—still hadn't, even after all these years—but she was positive of what she'd heard that night. *Growing... Like the Winchester Mystery House, Autumncrow is growing.*

Ellen made it home safely that night, but she never forgot the experience. It made her wary of ever again strolling through Autumncrow's moonlit streets alone. Ellen supposed this was a lesson every town local had to learn at some point. Tourists assumed Autumncrow Valley's ghostly yarns were all a ruse, but to those who spent their entire lives there—skeptical or otherwise—there was really no point in risking your life for a lonely nighttime stroll.

This is why, after The Little Bookshoppe of Curiosities

closed for business at six o'clock every weeknight, Ellen and Willow joined forces to close up shop and walk to their cars together. Not out of fear, but caution.

As they walked tonight, Willow shivered in her parka. "I don't know what you mean about it being humid. I'm so cold."

Ellen shook her head. "You're always cold. It's like you have a ghost hanging on your shoulders."

"Don't tell me that," Willow said, grinning to show Ellen she was only fibbing, but the smile faded into a look of exhaustion a second later.

"You need to get some rest, girl. You're way too young to be looking so tired," Ellen said.

A sophomore in high school, Willow always appeared beautifully mature for her age. The only thing longer than her wavy red locks were her legs, a trait that Ellen envied very much. But lately, Willow could have easily been mistaken for someone twice her age, and for all the wrong reasons. The poor girl looked like she hadn't had a decent night's rest in weeks.

"I'm fine." Willow changed the subject. "Want to grab a bite to eat at Spooky's Café? I'm starving."

Ellen's stomach rumbled at the thought of a grilled apple 'n cheese sandwich from Spooky's, but there was no time for dinner. "I wish I could. I have a long night of people scaring ahead of me. I'm manning the giant animatronic crocodile head again. You know, the one that made you piss your pants last week."

Willow nodded. "Yes."

Ellen shrugged. "The doors open at eight, but I doubt many will come tonight with the weather being so shitty. I hope it doesn't rain tomorrow or Luca isn't going to be happy. Halloween is our biggest night."

"It won't rain tomorrow. We never get rain on Halloween," Willow said, going out of her way to stomp on a dead leaf laying in the darkened doorway of Jack-o's Toys, shielded from the rain by a metal awning. The leaf crunched under Willow's foot, making Ellen grin in satisfaction; she loved the sound of cracking leaves.

"Has business been good, at least?" Willow asked.

"It's been great," Ellen replied. "Not that I've seen any of the money."

Willow paused midstride and gaped at Ellen. "Still?"

"Nothing yet," Ellen said, continuing her walk. She suddenly felt too embarrassed to meet her coworker's eyes. "But it's okay. Luca will pay me soon."

Willow quickened her pace to keep up with Ellen. "That's what you said last month."

"I know."

"You've been working on Luca's haunt for months now. You've earned your cut."

"It's not *Luca's* haunt. It's *our* haunt," Ellen countered. "It's just as much mine as it is his."

"Is it though?" Willow pressed, unfazed by Ellen's harsh tone. "I feel like he's taking advantage of you."

"He's not."

"Are you sure? With everything you've told me, it sounds like no one there respects you. You're working fulltime at the bookstore *and* working all night at the haunt. If I were you, I'd wave Luca goodbye."

Ellen shooed Willow's words with a flick of her wrist. "I've been doing this thing for ten years. I can't just up and quit."

Sure, Ellen had been flirting with the idea of quitting—more often than not—but every time she actually considered it, had planned on uttering the words that would end it all, she froze. Ellen knew what quitting really meant. Not only would she be walking away from the haunt, she would be walking away from Luca and Alvin, the guys she had been friends with since grade school. There would be no more trips to the drive-in, no more ghost hunts in the cemetery, no more game nights in Luca's basement. Instead, Ellen would stay home with her cats while Macy Collings took her place in the group.

Ellen wouldn't stand for that.

Sensing that it was time for a subject change, Willow said, "So, how's Tara the Android these days?"

Ellen sighed. "She's fine, I guess. We don't talk much."

That made Willow laugh, dissipating the tension in the air. "Well, as long as she doesn't freak you out anymore..."

"Nah, I'm pretty used to her by now," Ellen lied.

The duo walked past Undead Video, an old mom-and-pop video store that used its retro-horror appeal to keep business alive—or *undead*, as the name proclaimed. Ellen and Willow peeked through the window, past the scary movie posters and glowing neon signs, and saw the owner sitting inside. Bekah Ockerman was her name. Normally, she was busily shelving videos and assisting customers with their obscure movie requests, but tonight she was mindlessly flipping through a magazine. Turns out the weather had washed away her customers, too.

Ellen waved to Bekah and offered her a smile before moving on, passing Madame Tinkett's Sweets and stepping up to her car parked on the curb.

"Well, good luck tonight," Willow said, opening the driver's side door of her orange Volkswagen, parked just behind Ellen's Jeep. "Don't let Tara bite."

Ellen faked a laugh. "Get some rest tonight, okay? You'll need it for tomorrow."

She wasn't kidding. Come dawn, Autumncrow would be flooded with street vendors, business owners, and town committee workers, all banding together to prepare for the annual Halloween Carnival, an all-out monster bash that saw thousands of visitors from all over the country each and every year. It was a big deal for the community, and it also brought a lot of traffic to Dungeon of Death, so whether it rained or not, it would be a profitable night. Deep down, though, Ellen knew what Willow said was true; it wouldn't rain tomorrow. She couldn't recall a single Halloween where the weather was anything less than perfect.

Ellen started to get in her car when she paused. "Willow?"

Willow poked her head through her partially open door. "Yeah?"

"You're a good friend," Ellen said with a smile. "Happy Halloween."

3

The fog had started to dissipate by the time Ellen exited downtown and hit County Line Road. Dungeon of Death was a straight ten-minute shot from town, taking guests through spooky covered bridges with haunted histories, past cornfields aplenty. It was an atmospheric drive, though it was anything but relaxing; folks had to be on the lookout for crossing deer at all times. Last year, Ellen hadn't been watching the road carefully enough and smashed into what she assumed was a wolf. The creature was too large to be anything else. Her car had been totaled, yet somehow the wolf ran off through the fields, seemingly unscathed. *No fair,* Ellen had thought.

Looking across the cornfield now, Ellen could see the attraction from the road with the help of flickering strobe lights and an illuminated sign proclaiming *Dungeon of Death: Autumncrow's Scariest Haunt.* Blood dripped from the font. A gory horror film was being projected onto a giant screen for guests to watch as they waited in line. Ellen strained to see what movie Luca was showing tonight, but all she could make out was red. Lots and lots of red.

PHEEEEWMMM!

A bright flash of light shot across the road in a blur, right in front of Ellen's Jeep. It didn't collide with the car, but it sent a wave of force through the air, strong enough to push the front of the vehicle into a tailspin. Ellen didn't have a chance to scream, just clenched her teeth and rode this teacup until it came to a stop in the center of the road. It was then that she shouted, "NOT AGAIN!"

She took a moment to breathe, sending a signal from her head to her toes in hopes that she wouldn't detect any pain. As far as she could tell, she wasn't injured. She could only hope the same was true for her car.

She propped open the door and hopped out. Using the flashlight app on her phone, she circled her precious year-old Jeep and searched for any signs of damage.

Fine. Everything was fine. Her insurance company could

rest easy.

Now it was time to figure out what the hell had darted in front of her car. It definitely wasn't an animal. That thing, whatever it was, had been glowing bright as a beacon.

A drone, maybe? People often flew those out here to utilize the open air, but only during the day. The idea of someone flying a drone on a dark, rainy night seemed unlikely. And while Ellen knew next to squat about drones, she didn't believe any could create enough force to spin a car. No, the drone idea wasn't plausible.

For a moment, Ellen considered that Alvin might be behind all this, that he was hiding among the towering cornstalks, giggling as he always did after pulling a good one. But Ellen had known Alvin since they were kids; he could be a pain, sure, but he would never put Ellen's life in danger. She was lucky to walk away unscathed.

Striding past her car, Ellen gazed over the cornfield bordering the right side of the road, in the direction of Dungeon of Death. Whatever the light had been, it had to be out there somewhere in the field. Ellen peered through the darkness, shining her phone's light over the rows. She could make out a narrow path cut through the corn. Each stalk had been whacked in half, the smoke from their serrated tips mingling with the fog. It was as if each stalk had been chopped in two with a fiery scythe.

Ellen stepped off the road and came to a stop at the edge of the cornfield. The path, she could see, stretched deep into the field, the end too far for her light to reach. Darkness stared back at her, daring her to investigate.

She wasn't going to. As curious as Ellen was, it would be stupid to go any further. She didn't know what was out there, what had knocked her car for a loop. As slim as the odds were, she was beginning to suspect that it was a meteor—what else would be hot enough to pop this cornfield? The stalks were literally sizzling. If this was true, who knows what contaminants she could be inhaling this very moment.

"Meteor shit," Ellen muttered, referencing one of her favorite horror films.

She hopped in her car and sped off, following the curving road until she reached the parking lot of the haunt. A few people were already waiting at the entrance, umbrellas held over their heads, though the rain had mostly come to a stop. Luca's movie of choice was *The Gruesome Twosome* directed by Herschell Gordon Lewis. The guests seemed uncomfortable.

Ellen climbed out of her car and waved to the guests before walking around the building to the staff entrance where scarers would be applying makeup and prosthetics, transforming themselves into Autumncrow's creepiest creatures. Before entering, Ellen paused and looked toward the cornfield. There was nothing unusual about it; no mysterious lights, no alien beasts. But the feeling of being watched was present, making Ellen's skin prickle with chills.

Call for Mommy, you little shit!

Pushing the door open, Ellen was welcomed inside by an energetic cast and crew, each one eager to scare the pants off anybody who dared enter their Dungeon of Death. Ellen forced a smile, tried to convince herself that the feeling of dread rising in her gut was nothing more than the result of being in an accident. But she couldn't shake the fear that something was hiding out there in the fields, something far more dangerous than meteor shit.

4

It hadn't been here before.

Weaving through the cornstalks, the creature was mystified by many things—the terrain; the feeling of moisture in the air, low and heavy; the odd sensation of gravity that rendered travel more difficult. Among the stars, the thing flowed freely, without struggle. Here, it had to fight against Earth's pull in order to remain airborne, lest it be dragged to the ground again and again.

Exhausted, the thing nestled into the cornstalks, enjoying the slight rise and fall of the soil. This pulse, undetectable by humans, was immediately apparent to the thing's heightened senses. Whatever lived in the soil—in the air itself—had called the creature here, invited it to this sleepy little town. The thing felt welcomed, embraced, loved. Hungry.

Never before had the creature visited a planet containing this much blood. The smell was everywhere, closing in from all directions.

Hungry... So very hungry...

Soon enough, the thing would feed. After all, where there was blood, there was a host. Once it gained possession, the thing would be able to drink until its thirst was satiated, and then drink some more. Driven by its growing appetite, the creature rose into the air, a black mist hanging above the cornfield, and pushed toward that sweet smell of delicious liquid life.

There was movement to the left, and then a voice spoke. "Okay, see you tomorrow night." The words were foreign, but that hardly mattered. What mattered was the lifeblood fueling those words. The creature exited the cornfield and hovered over the front lawn of Dungeon of Death. The spotlights illuminating the billboard-sized sign were being unplugged. Vehicles containing the scent of blood were moving away.

A dark-skinned girl climbed in her own vehicle and followed the others down the curving country road. The thing recognized this human. She was the first it had seen upon crashing to Earth. It would have possessed her, too, had it not been so tired.

The creature was about to follow the departing vehicles when it stopped. Another smell caught its attention, a mysterious one with a vague resemblance to blood. Intrigued, the thing followed the scent toward Dungeon of Death and drifted through one of its outer walls. It found itself in a dark hallway, absent of human activity. Still, that smell...

Winding through the corridors, the thing discovered nothing of interest. There were some severed arms reaching from the walls but, strangely enough, they lacked the scent the creature craved, aside from being entirely unpossessable. Useless human carnage.

It moved on, the smell growing stronger and stronger until the thing discovered the source; a small black box of some kind. Hovering over the box like a storm cloud, the creature enjoyed the strange aroma. Yes, it did smell faintly of blood, but there was something else. Glycerin-based fluids, maybe? Or some kind of mineral oil?

Curiously, the creature gave the black box a slight nudge, then another, harder this time. It was then that a thick cloud of smoke bellowed from the box, instantly covering the floor with fog. The substance pushed the creature back-

ward, knocking it into a blond human female that stood against the wall. As soon as it made impact with the girl, she began to move, singing a high-pitched mechanical song.

"I feel fantastic... hey hey hey heeeeey..."

The creature cowered in fear. Had it owned a mouth, it surely would have screamed. But sadly, it did not. Only Earth's children had the privilege of unleashing a cry to control their escalating terror. Taking a moment to collect itself, the creature eyed the odd woman. It felt embarrassment at having been startled by a pathetic human being, a species useful for food and food alone. Aggravated, the thing lunged at the woman, bumping into her. She fell to the ground with a loud clatter but continued her odd tune.

"Run run run run..."

Creepy... the thing thought. The human species was a strange one, but at least they were tasty. With immense excitement, the smoky creature zoomed forward, entering the singing girl's body and initiating control.

Tara the Android sprung to life.

5

The streets of Autumncrow were alive with activity. Costumed children poured into town from all corners, bags already bursting with trick-or-treat goodies, though it was barely six o'clock. They ran about in pure delight, throwing their allowance money at food vendors serving every variety of pumpkin- and apple-flavored desserts. Other children tried their hands at spooky carnival games or waited in line at Mayor Sherman's Haunted Courthouse or participated in the town square pumpkin carving contest.

Even the adults were in the Halloween spirit. Each were dressed in elaborate outfits in hopes that they would win best costume. It wasn't until a man in a headless horseman getup came galloping into town on a black steed, waving about a flaming jack-o'-lantern, that the contestants realized they would not be taking home the grand prize.

At dusk, the harvest moon climbed a ladder of stars and shined upon the scene below. This was All Hallows' as it should be. In Autumncrow, you didn't have to look back on your childhood memories of Halloween in sad remembrance. Here, you could live out those memories once again, or create new ones with your children. Halloween wasn't dead, you just needed to know where to find it.

Ellen watched the Halloween Carnival from the front window of The Little Bookshoppe of Curiosities and smiled. While she typically despised large crowds, she couldn't help but fall in love with the kooky characters this event brought to her hometown. Halloween was a magical night, made even more enchanting by the passionate people uniting on the streets.

"Hey, Ellie, can you give me a hand?" Willow asked, interrupting Ellen's thoughts. "I know you're off the clock, but..."

Turning, Ellen saw Willow walking across the store, balancing a hefty stack of hardcovers. "I thought I could do it on my own," she added.

Ellen laughed and took half of the books from Willow. "You could have used the cart."

"I know," Willow said, dropping the books on the table that their guest would be stationed at, an author by the name of Jack Rosenlove. Willow picked up a copy of the book and used her index finger to trace the cover's embossed jack-o'-lantern. *Autumncrow: A Dark History,* the title read.

"That should sell well tonight," Ellen said, looking toward the entrance of the store. People were already flooding inside to take their seats for the Q&A and signing, even though it didn't start for another hour. Douglas Hanlon, the bookstore owner, hurried in among the crowd and nodded to the girls.

"Sorry I'm late," he said, taking off toward his office. "Ellen, clock out!" he called over his shoulder.

"Already did," Ellen mumbled. She shared an eyeroll with Willow. "Of all days to be late."

"You're going to be late, too, if you don't get going," Willow said. "Good luck tonight."

"You too, kiddo." Ellen hugged Willow. "Maybe we can grab lunch tomorrow. And do a little shopping around town."

Willow pulled away, beaming. "Really? I thought you'd have to help close down the dungeon."

"Hell no. After tonight, I'm telling Luca to pay up and eat shit."

Ellen meant it, too. She'd spent the previous night replaying Willow's words in her head, encouraging her to part ways with Luca and Alvin. The more Ellen thought about it, the more she realized that her friendship with the guys was drying up, much like a boyfriend you stay with month after month, not because you're in love with him but because you know no other way of life. You can fight against the universe all you want, but it will continue to pull you away until you haven't the energy to hold on any longer.

Ellen supposed the same could be true for platonic friends. It was time to say goodbye, and that was okay. New friends could be made, like the one standing right in front of her.

"I'm proud of you," Willow said, giving Ellen a light punch on the shoulder.

"Well, I haven't done it yet! Don't put more pressure on me," Ellen joked. "Anyway, see you at Spooky's tomorrow, okay?"

Ellen made her way through the crowded store onto the equally crowded sidewalk. She walked in the direction of her Jeep, parked several blocks away on a neighborhood street, and took in the sights and sounds of the carnival. The scent of caramel and peanuts wafted from a nearby candy apple stand. She considered buying one for the road but decided against it when she saw how long the line was. It would make a sticky mess in the car anyway.

When Ellen found her Jeep, she rolled down the windows to let in the crisp nighttime air and started toward Dungeon of Death. The haunt wound up being a hit last night, selling over five hundred tickets. That amount may be tripled tonight with it being Halloween, especially when you factored in the beautiful weather. Willow had been right; the drizzle yesterday paved the way for Halloween's orange reign.

6

Macy Collings was the first to arrive at Dungeon of Death. It was six o'clock and the haunt wouldn't open until nine. Luca thought opening later would give guests (and himself) more time to enjoy the carnival, but Macy decided to come early to repair her vampiress dress. It had been badly torn last night, giving an elderly woman and her ten-year-old granddaughter an eyeful of ass. It wasn't Macy's proudest moment.

She stepped into the staffroom and noticed the off-key tune of a girl's singing voice before she even turned on the lights.

"I feel fantastic..." it vocalized.

Alvin's stupid mannequin, Macy thought. *Did he really leave that thing running all night and day?*

She strode through the staffroom and opened the door leading into the haunt, peeking her head into a dark hallway. "Tara, you creepy bitch," she called. "Shut your trap before I shut it for you."

"Run run run run..." Tara's voice echoed through the hall.

"Have it your way then," Macy replied with a shudder. In all honesty, while Macy had been teasing Ellie about her fear of the mannequin all October long, she agreed that Tara the Android was one freaky chick. She even thought about taking Tara to the dump at one point, disposing of her altogether. But she worried the others would find out she was responsible for Tara's disappearance, and she'd be outed as being an even bigger wimp than Ellen Reid. Nah, Macy could handle Tara the Android just fine.

Finding a light switch hidden behind a mechanical werewolf prop, Macy flicked it upward, bathing the hall in a purple neon glow, followed by the ticking of a strobe light. It made for an eerier atmosphere, but at least she could see the path. Macy walked through the hallway, pressing herself against one wall to avoid the rubber severed arms reaching for her. Tara's song grew louder as Macy drew nearer.

At the end of the hall hung a black curtain, shielding the room beyond. When Macy pushed the curtain aside, a thick cloud of fog barreled out.

"What—What the...?" Macy Collings attempted to wave the vapor away from her face, but more fog instantly took its place. Pushing her way into the room, Macy located the fog machine and unplugged it from the wall socket. "Who the hell left this thing running?" she wondered aloud.

"You feel fantastic... hey hey hey heeeeeey..."

Macy shrieked and spun around. Tara the Android's voice sounded like it had come from right behind Macy, but she couldn't see a thing; the fog was so thick it blinded her completely. Not only that, but Macy couldn't hear Tara anymore. The room was completely quiet. Had the batteries finally died?

Tick tick tick tick tick...

The tapping of high-heeled shoes sounded to Macy's right. She gasped and shuffled away from the sound, only to get her own heels tangled in the fog machine's electrical cord. Macy sailed to the ground, hitting with a *thump.*

"Ow! Shit!" she cried.

Reaching for the cord, she attempted to untangle her feet, but she still couldn't see a single thing. Her heart raced. Her hands trembled. Someone... someone was in the room with her. Macy could hear them now, moving about in the fog, the ticking of their heels bouncing off the walls.

"Who's there?" Macy called. "I swear to God, whoever is in here, I'll kill you!"

The tapping stopped. Silence.

Teeth chattering, Macy finally freed her feet and stood, peering into the fog. All was still. So very still.

"Screw this," Macy whispered. Keeping her eyes locked on the space ahead, she backed up until she collided with a wall caked in spiderwebs. *You've got this,* Macy assured herself. She would follow the wall until she reached the exit, then she would hightail it out of here.

Before she could take another step, however, two white lights illuminated the fog in one corner of the room. The lights, hovering side-by-side about an inch apart, were circular and harsh, making Macy squint.

"What—? Who—?" Macy stammered.

Suddenly, the lights raced toward her, accompanied by that *click click click* of running heels. Macy issued a raspy cry as Tara the Android's face rushed out of the fog, illuminated by the white glow of her eyes. Tara's hands shot upward in a Frankenstein's Monster pose, its fingers wrapping around Macy's neck.

Macy couldn't comprehend what was happening, but whatever it was, it just wasn't possible. This couldn't be real. A special effect maybe, something Alvin had rigged up.

But as Tara the Android opened her rubber mouth and dug her plastic teeth into Macy's jugular, she realized too late that this wasn't one of Alvin's jump scares, and neither was the blood spurting from her wound. Macy screamed as the creature inside Tara basked in the sweet aroma of syrupy blood.

7

As soon as Ellen stepped into the Dungeon of Death staffroom, she knew something was wrong. Macy Colling's car was stationed in the parking lot, but she was nowhere to be seen. Her costume remained where it had been placed last night before closing, hanging on the clothes rack, still torn and in need of repair.

"Macy?" Ellen said.

No reply.

Glancing around, she finally noticed the open door leading into the haunted attraction. A strobe light flickered inside. Carefully, Ellen stepped toward the door and poked her head in. The lighted hall stretched on, dead ending at the drawn black curtain. A hint of fog floated in the air.

"Macy? What are you doing?" Ellen called.

Still, no reply.

It could be that Macy was too far inside to hear, but a feeling of dread—the same one Ellen felt last night after seeing the white light on the road—made Ellen's skin stand on end. She pulled her cellphone from her purse and found Luca's number. He picked up after three rings.

"Hey," he shouted. A drone of voices could be heard in the background, as well as the tinny beat of "You Can't Get Him—Frankenstein" by The Castle Kings.

"Hi," Ellen said. "Are you with Macy?"

"No," Luca replied. "I'm at the carnival with Alvin. We're about to head over to the dungeon."

"Okay..." Ellen trailed off. "Well, Macy's car is here, but she's not in the staffroom."

"Yeah, she said she was coming in early to fix her dress."

"I know, but she's not here," Ellen repeated. "And her dress hasn't been fixed. And the door to the haunt is open, but she's not answering when I call for her."

"Yeah...?" Luca said, unfazed.

"And something seems wrong," Ellen finished.

"Damn, what is with you lately?" he said. "You never used to be scared of anything, but ever since we brought Tara into the haunt, you've been a mess."

Ellen's face wrinkled in annoyance at the sudden attack. "Hey, that's not true. And this has nothing to do with that stupid mannequin. I'm worried about Macy."

Luca burst into laughter. "Since when do you care about Macy?"

Ellen shook her head. "I don't! I mean... I just feel like something weird is going on."

There was a pause on the other line. Luca and Alvin's murmuring voices were unintelligible under the loud music. Finally, Luca said, "God, this place is packed. We'll be there in a half hour, okay?"

The call ended.

Ellen groaned in disgust. *What is with those guys?* she wondered. Luca wanted to turn this on her, say that Tara's presence had changed her in some way, but that couldn't be further from the truth. It was Luca and Alvin that had changed.

Thinking of Luca's patronizing words, Ellen said, "I'm not scared of *shit.*" She threw her cell on the cushion of a nearby loveseat and entered the Dungeon of Death.

8

It wasn't working.

In possession of the mannequin, the creature munched on the flesh of Macy's neck, crunching through every vein and muscle until Tara's plastic teeth struck bone. The delicious smell of blood filled the air, igniting the thing's senses. Hungryhungryhungryhungry... *it thought. And hungry it would remain.*

Something was wrong with this vessel. First off, it had no capability of taste, no way of savoring the wonders that blood had to offer. Secondly, this girl's body had yet to ingest a single drop of the liquid. Whatever entered Tara's mouth fell right back out, splashing Macy's dead eyes with her own ichor.

The creature was beginning to suspect that this 'girl' it had possessed wasn't a girl at all, wasn't even human. It had been fooled again!

A gasp sounded from behind the creature, tugging it out of its feeding frenzy. In a 180-degree spin, Tara's head swiveled around to face the entryway of the room. A girl stood there, holding a hand to her gaping mouth, eyes wide. This was the same girl the thing had seen on the road last night. She had narrowly escaped possession before, but the human wouldn't be so lucky this time.

In its excitement, the creature began to glow inside the mannequin's body, a bright pulsing light that emanated from Tara's eye sockets, shining onto Ellen's terrified face.

"Run run run run..." *Tara sang.*

9

Ellen ran. She powered her way through the Dungeon of Death, ignoring the pain of being whacked in the face by dozens of severed arms reaching from the walls. All the while, the nightmarish voice of Tara floated after her, begging her to feel fantastic. Demanding that she run.

Oh God oh no oh please oh God, Ellen chanted in her mind.

This couldn't be happening. What she saw in that room, the mannequin kneeling over Macy's corpse, feasting on her blood, gore dripping from its jaws—none of that was real. *Wasn't real wasn't real wasn't real...* and yet, Ellen couldn't force herself to turn around, couldn't confirm her suspicion that this was all a Halloween prank. Deep down, she knew it wasn't.

She rushed through the staffroom and out the exit, feeling the cold All Hallows' air on her sweaty skin. The breeze rustled the dead cornstalks nearby as the moon observed Ellen's desperate retreat.

Reaching the locked driver's side door of her Jeep, Ellen remembered that her keys were tucked inside the front pocket of her purse, which she had conveniently left in the staffroom. She faced the haunt, pausing long enough to see Tara the Android burst through the staffroom door. The mannequin's jaw and sweater were stained crimson. Its movements were disjointed, hands stretching toward Ellen in feral desperation.

Ellen screamed and turned away from those haunting headlight eyes. The only thing she could think to do was run into the cornfield and find a place to hide until her friends arrived. There was nowhere else to go.

The cornstalks were rigid, their leaves sharp as blades. They sliced Ellen's arms and face, but she didn't dare stop running. Her nightmare maintained its pursuit. Its song grew closer and closer with every passing second.

"I feel fantastic... hey hey heeeey..."

Ellen's icy lungs felt fit to burst. *Please make it stop,* she begged silently. *Make it stop!*

As if in answer to Ellie's prayer, Tara's voice ceased mid-song. Other than Ellen's jagged, wheezing breaths, the night was as silent as a tomb. The wind no longer whispered among the cornstalks. Bats no longer screeched overhead. Even the crickets postponed their harmony.

Ellen spun in circles, terrified to leave her back turned to any spot for more than a second. The thing could be anywhere, waiting to spring out from behind.

A low rumbling sound gave her pause. Peering through the cornstalks, she spotted two glowing lights. At first, she assumed these were the bright eyes of the mannequin moving through the field, but then she heard the unmistakable lyrics of Michael Jackson's "Thriller" floating toward her.

"Luca... Alvin..." she whispered. These glowing white orbs were the headlights of Luca's Ford Mustang zipping down County Line Road.

Ellen took off in the direction of the lights, her feet pumping the ground at a speed she didn't know she was capable of. *Yes, almost there. Almost over! Safe... Safe!*

She thought too soon.

As she came to the edge of the field, pushing aside the last two cornstalks that would grant her access to the country road, Ellen was met with the blood covered face of Tara the Android. Her eyes grew brighter and brighter, bathing its new host in unholy light.

Blinded, Ellen felt something enter her mouth, her nose, her ears. It writhed inside her chest, pushing against her organs and ribcage. It flowed into her bloodstream. It expanded into her brain, pulsing in her temples.

A deep, raspy voice spoke from somewhere inside Ellen's head. Four syllables, nothing more. The words were foreign—*alien*—but somehow, Ellen understood the thing's damning message: *"Follow me in..."*

The lights went out. At the same moment, something snapped deep within Ellen's stomach, a root being yanked from the ground. She was left to float in darkness, untethered from herself and everything she knew in life. All around, unseen hands began to grab at her arms and legs, pulling her deeper and deeper. And the sound!—that rhythmic hammering beat. Ellen recognized it immediately.

Growing... Autumncrow is growing.

Ellen was dragged into eternity, screaming.

10

Tara the Android collapsed to the ground, a useless pile of gears and plastic. Standing over the rubble was what used to be Ellen Reid, a fun-loving woman who adored her cats, one who enjoyed grilled apple 'n cheese sandwiches from Spooky's Cafe and movie nights with friends and pulpy horror novels and old Twilight Zone *episodes. The thing now inhabiting Ellen's body could feel the strong beat of her heart. It was a good heart. This human was undeserving of such a fate. But in the end, nothing was fair in Autumncrow Valley.*

A short distance away, a light popped on, illuminating a sign that read Dungeon of Death: Autumncrow's Scariest Haunt. *The thing saw two humans enter the building, carrying with them the intoxicating elixir of pulsing life.*

Following the scent, Ellen walked along the road toward Dungeon of Death, a vampire queen ready for her grand finale.

CRYP-TV

As 13-year-old Allen Morrisby waited alone in the darkness of Kilgore Cemetery, biting his lip impatiently and shivering with the cold, he couldn't help but feel a sense of disappointment with this supposed mystical and ancient night.

Halloween was the most important of the year. The streets should have been bursting with children, running from house to house until dawn, filling pillowcase after pillowcase with every kind of candy imaginable and wreaking havoc on the houses that refused to hand it over. There should have been a monster movie marathon at the local theater in town with free hotdogs and rigged seats and monsters roaming the aisles. The library should have been open until midnight, performing ghost stories for scared children around a faux campfire, their tired parents drinking hot cider and wondering when—*if*—this night would ever end.

There should have been pumpkin carving contests in the town square and haunted hayrides and chainsaws and... the dead!—the dead wondering the earth in droves, stumbling about everywhere you looked. Witches should have been cackling on broomsticks overhead while vampires feasted on the blood of virgins in black alleyways.

This is how things were in Autumncrow Valley, the small Ohio town Allen lived in until last year. Yes, there were zombies, witches, and vampires there, too. At least, that's what Allen would have told you. There were just too many weird occurrences in that town to make you a skeptic. Rumored haunted houses, UFO sightings, dead family members showing up for dinner, missing children, a dark and twisted forest said to be the home of lost souls; you name it, Autumncrow had it. In the end, however, it was the missing children reports that made Allen's parents pack up and move one town over to Kilgore.

This won't be so bad, Allen had thought, trying to stay positive about the whole thing. Kilgore was a small town after all, so it wouldn't be too different from what Allen was used to. And being only a few miles away from Autumncrow, it was a short ten-minute drive to see his old friends... though his parents forbid it. *"They* can come visit *you,"* Allen's mother had said. And that was that.

His friends were sad to see him go, but "Hey," Joey Tunkle had said during lunch on Allen's last day, "the name of the town sounds like the title of an old slasher film. How bad can it be?"

Bad.

Kilgore was anything but a slasher film. It was a small town, yes, but it lacked the sense of adventure that Autumncrow had. In other words, it was boring. Even on this night, the greatest, spookiest night of all, Kilgore was about as fun as chewing unpopped corn kernels. For instance, all the kids in his homeroom laughed at Allen when he asked what they'd be dressing up as for trick-or-treat.

"You go trick-or-treating?"

"What are you, five?"

"Are you a baby, Allen? Do you watch Disney movies?"

"Invalid argument, Kevin. Everyone watches Disney movies now."

"No way, Judy, not me!"

So. No one trick-or-treated here. Great. What was Allen supposed to do on Halloween night?

"Please let me trick-or-treat in Autumncrow," Allen had begged his parents the night before. "Please! Just this one night with my friends and that's it. I'll never ask again."

"Allen, stop it," his mother scolded. "We've told you over and over. That town has become too dangerous, especially on Halloween. Why don't your friends come here for beggar's night?"

"They won't want to do that!" exclaimed Allen breathlessly. "This place is depressing. Its—its...Mom. Dad. Look. No one decorates here. The stores don't even sell pumpkins, for Cthulhu's sake. The trees don't even know its Autumn! The kids in my grade don't trick-or-treat either. And the kids who do—the 'babies'—are only staying out until eight o'clock tomorrow. Barely. And after that, all the porch lights will go out and everyone will go to bed and what are we supposed to do then?"

His mother sighed. "There's always Trunk-or-Treat at the Methodist Church." Even as she said it, she knew it was a sad alternative.

Allen shook his head. "If my friends came here, it would ruin their Halloween and it would be all my fault."

"If they were your true friends, they wouldn't blame you," his dad chimed in gruffly from his recliner.

"Then they'll blame *you!*" Allen yelled and stormed off to his room.

Allen's comment didn't make his parents any more accepting of the Autumncrow idea. Basically, it was an "enough is enough, that is that" kind of situation.

Halloween is ruined, Allen thought. *My night... ruined.*

Then came the dare. It always starts with a dare, doesn't it?

"Hey, Adam! C'mere. We wanna talk to you about somethin'." These words had been spoken by none other than Daryl Lowly. He was sitting at a lunch table with his two comrades. Allen didn't know their names, but it didn't matter. They had forfeited their identities and sold their souls when they became part of Daryl's ranks.

"My name is *Allen,* not Adam," Allen said.

"You see someone who cares?" Daryl sneered. "I told you to come over here."

Allen was only sitting an arm's length away from the goons, so he didn't see why he had to go any nearer, but being afraid of very little, he scooted close enough for Daryl to drape a skinny arm around his shoulders. The kid smelled like cigarettes and old gym bleachers.

"We was hearing you like weird stuff."

"I don't think what I like is weird," Allen muttered.

Daryl flicked one of the enamel pins on Allen's jacket. It was a handmade pin showing an evil jack-o'-lantern brandishing a bloody butcher knife with its viney arms. "From where I'm sitting, it's pretty weird," Daryl said. "And with you being from that spook town, I'm sure you noticed

Kilgore is very... not weird."

"I've noticed," Allen said.

"Well, what if I was to tell you not everything is normal in this neck of the woods?"

This caught Allen's attention. "I'm listening."

Daryl went on to tell of rumors surrounding Kilgore Cemetery, more specifically rumors of a particular crypt. It used to be a popular hangout spot for teens, Daryl had explained, until the police shut it down. Now voices could be heard drifting over the cemetery at night, most notably on Halloween.

Allen threw Daryl a bored glare. "That's it? Phantom voices? That's all you've got?"

One of Daryl's goons—a large girl who was no more than fourteen but already had knuckle tattoos—gave Allen an angry punch to the arm. "He's not done telling the story yet, idiot."

"Let's not get violent, Hanna," Daryl said. "As a matter of fact, there *is* more to the story. A bunch of kids has gone in that crypt since the police boarded it up. Broke in through the back. They wanted to see where those voices was coming from. But they never came out. They went missing."

Missing? *Missing?* Allen could have screamed. The whole reason his parents had moved him here in the first place was because of the missing kids in Autumncrow. And come to find out, this town was no different.

Had his parents known? Surely they would have researched this place before deciding to settle here. All you had to do was look at the town to know that the crime rate was high. There were abandoned buildings everywhere, covered in graffiti. Trash littered every roadside. The people were rough and mean. The most popular hangout spot was the nearest Walmart. Nearly every person over the age of thirty had missing teeth. And their grammar was horrible. It seemed obvious to Allen that kids could go missing here.

Thinking back on it now, hours later, Allen could feel the anger rising again, anger at his parents, anger at Kilgore, anger at the fact that he was now standing alone in a dark cemetery on Halloween night with no one to talk to.

Where are those goons anyway? Allen looked around, seeing nothing but moss-covered tombstones and dozens of crypts. Other than the dead people under his feet and the occasional bat diving through the air for a tasty moth, Allen was the only one around.

An owl called from somewhere nearby. Allen peered into the tree branches overhead, limbs swaying in the chilly night breeze like arms playing tag with unseen spirits. Allen couldn't see the owl from where he stood but it was probably up there now, staring down at him from the darkness with large spooky eyes.

Believe it or not, this cheered Allen up a little bit. Even if Daryl and his friends didn't show up, at least Allen could say he spent the night in a creepy graveyard instead of sitting on the couch with his parents. After all, this cemetery was the only place in Kilgore that reminded Allen of home.

CRACK!

A tree branch snapped from somewhere behind. If Allen was a normal kid, he may have jumped out of his skin at the sound, but Allen never found breaking tree branches to be very scary. He turned around casually and there stood

Daryl and his friends, leaning against one of the graveyard's many towering monuments.

"I thought you guys were going to stand me up," Allen said.

"We thought you was gonna chicken out, so we took our time," Daryl said.

"Well, here I am." Allen crossed his arms.

"Right. Follow us. The crypt is this way." All four kids tromped through the cemetery, the flashlights of their phones illuminating the way. "You won't be needing this," Daryl said as he snatched the phone out of Allen's hand. Allen didn't put up a fight. He did not want these guys to think he was scared to be without his phone. Which he definitely wasn't. But in an hour's time, when his mother realized he still wasn't home, she would undoubtedly try to call his cell. And when she didn't get an answer, both she and his father would come searching. And that *did* scare Allen, just a little bit.

A cloud covered the moon overhead, robbing the landscape of all natural light. One of the Daryls, a tall, lanky boy wearing a dirty beanie, stopped in mid-step. "I've never been out here at night before. Are you sure you know where we're going, Daryl?"

"Of course I do, Todd," Daryl snapped without stopping his march through the high grass. "Don't doubt me."

The small quiver in Todd's voice made the corners of Allen's lips curve upward. This always happened when he sensed someone else's fear. Call him a sadist all you will, but Allen found it hilarious when others yelped or squirmed in terror. Screams were music to Allen's ears, but it was even better when *he* was the organist, when *he* was the one composing a symphony of fear. And he hoped to high hope for the opportunity to scare these tough guys by the end of the night.

That was the whole reason he had agreed to this dare in the first place. Allen didn't like Daryl or his friends. He saw how they treated others. They were mean and rude and obviously had plans to terrify Allen tonight in some way. But they wouldn't. He would play their game just long enough to turn the tables on them. He didn't know how yet, but he'd have plenty of time to brainstorm once inside the crypt. Whatever the plan, it would be easy to scare them. Hanna and Todd were already getting spooked by the dark, and Daryl, though seemingly fearless, wouldn't be as difficult to crack as it appeared.

"Daryl..." Todd spoke again, his voice wobbly.

"Shut up. We're already here. See?" Daryl shined his light on the crypt in front of them.

The first word that sprung to Allen's mind upon seeing the crypt was not the first word that came to the other kids' minds. They thought: *Creepy.* Allen thought: *Awesome.* The moon broke through the clouds above, casting a soft blue glow on the face of the crypt, illuminating each eerie detail. It was a small sepulcher, just large enough to rest a cadaver or two, but it stood tall with sharp vaulted roofing supported by thick pillars on either side of the wrought iron door. Years of algae haunted every surface.

But what really stood out to Allen and the others was not the spooky nature of the vault but the freshly carved jack-o'-lantern grinning at them from the stone steps leading to the entrance. It flickered in the night, casting orangey candle-light upon each of their confused faces.

"Who put that there?" Hanna asked.

"I dunno," Daryl answered. "Looks like someone else has been here tonight."

The group stared at the jack-o'-lantern in silence. All that could be heard was the wind rustling its fingers through the unkempt grass. No phantom voices though. And no rattling chains.

Allen rolled his eyes. This must have been the first part in a series of jokes leading to some big punchline. A pumpkin, however, was a poor attempt at scaring Allen; he didn't find them to be scary at all. On the other hand, he thought it was a nice way to set the atmosphere.

"So, are we going to do this thing or what?" Allen asked.

Daryl tossed Allen a dirty look. "Fine. This way."

"But what about the pumpkin, man?" Hanna intervened. "That's kinda weird. Whoever put it there might still be around. Or maybe it was the ghost who haunts the crypt. The one who took Margaret Edgar and Bryce Kugler and—"

Allen just about died laughing. "You guys are too much. Seriously, let's get on with it. You're just wasting my time. I mean, even if there were a hundred ghosts in that crypt—and I hope there are—I'm from Autumncrow. It's nothing I haven't experienced already, trust me. Try to scare me all you want, but I can take it."

Daryl sneered at Hanna and Todd, his eyes no different than the fire inside that jack-o'-lantern. "It's good to know what a bunch of losers I have as friends. Makes me think I should reconsider who's worthy of being in this here group."

Both Todd and Hanna cast their eyes to the ground in a

mix of shame and fear. Daryl looked to Allen with a kind of newfound respect. "This way."

Allen followed Daryl to the back of the crypt. He could see that each window was half-heartedly boarded up, not enough to keep out a rodent let alone danger-seeking teenagers. Daryl grabbed one of the two-by-fours and pulled it free from a window with barely any effort. Behind the board was a window totally free of glass or iron bars. This must have been the entrance Daryl was talking about, the one everyone used to break in through.

"You can climb through here," he said. "You remember what you have to do, yeah?"

"It's not exactly difficult," Allen said. "I go in, I wait until midnight to see if anything happens, then you guys come and get me. Simple."

"Nah." Daryl shook his head. "You can wait until 12:30 instead. All the scary stuff happens at midnight, so you at least wanna stay for that."

"Fine. 12:30 then." *An extra half-hour of Mom and Dad wondering if I snuck off to Autumncrow to be with my friends after all.* Allen knew that's what they would think. He wouldn't be surprised if they were calling up his friends' parents right now. *"Have you seen our Allen? Have you seen our boy?!"*

Allen pushed the thought aside and propped himself up on the marbled windowsill. Daryl helped out by giving Allen's butt a hard shove. He toppled through the opening, clattering on top of a tomb resting just below the window.

"Ow," Allen gasped, rubbing his elbows.

Daryl snorted. "Good luck, dude. If you go missing, thanks for the iPhone." He chucked a small flashlight at

Allen before bounding away from the window, going God knows where. Probably to set up the next big scare of the night. *How will they ever top that pumpkin?* Allen wondered dryly. *Could it possibly get any scarier than that?*

Pushing himself off the tomb, Allen issued a quick apology to whoever was inside, just in case they were thinking of issuing a noise complaint. Allen, unlike some kids, respected the dead, though he didn't think anyone was haunting this place, at least not tonight. If a ghost had any sense at all, it would go to Autumncrow for its Halloween celebration. It wouldn't be floating around in this lonely old crypt. Right?

As if on cue, Allen heard a voice. At least, he thought it was a voice.

He stood in the middle of the chilly vault, unmoving, listening carefully. Nothing now. No sound at all, in fact. Allen originally assumed it would be noisy in the crypt, with a constant *drip-drip* of water echoing off the walls and the ticking of little rat feet colliding with the stone floor. Instead, it was as if all sound had suddenly vanished. Not even the wind could be heard whistling outside.

Strange... but there had been a voice a moment ago. It was faint and muffled, but it was here. Somewhere. Was it just one of the Daryls goofing around outside? Probably. That, or they were already trying to spook Allen. Their pacing was all off. They at least needed to wait an hour or two before trying anything, to give Allen a chance to settle in before the big "BOO!" In Allen's experience of scaring people, he knew timing was key, even if you had to wait for hours on end cramped inside a tiny closet. In the end, patience was what made the scare all the more satisfying.

The Daryls clearly had little experience in such things.

"Nice try, guys," Allen said. "But you'll have to do better than that."

He picked up the flashlight that Daryl had thrown to him and shined it on his surroundings. It looked like the interior of any other tiny crypt. Twin tombs sat parallel to the narrow walkway in between. The epitaph etched into the stone of the first tomb read:

Autumn Crow
Beloved wife and friend.
August 15, 1791 - October 31, 1820.

"Autumn *what?*" Allen—feeling like Indiana Jones on the brink of discovering hidden riches—turned and surveyed the second tomb.

Abraham Crow
Cherished husband and storyteller.
His head was a pumpkin with a blackbird inside.
February 25, 1785 – November 18, 1851.

Scratching his head, Allen read the carving over and over. He had spent his whole life in Autumncrow, heard the story of the Crows told countless times. But this didn't make any sense.

Tourists assumed the town was named after a Native American chief or tribe, but that wasn't the case. According to legend, Native people stayed far away from the land under the belief that it was cursed. It was a man by the name of Abraham Crow who founded the town in 1810, naming it after his newly wedded wife, Autumn. Ten years later, Autumn became ill and passed away. Abraham lived on into his sixties before being laid to rest in Autumncrow Cemetery. Allen had visited Abraham's crypt countless times, had even gone there to read or do his homework when he needed a quiet place. So how was it that Abraham Crow was buried here in Kilgore Cemetery when he was already buried in the next town over?

As for Autumn, why wasn't she buried in Autumncrow? Allen had seen the stone monument that was placed there in her honor—a sad looking woman in a long flowing dress standing in the middle of the cemetery—but he had never been able to find her actual grave. Until now.

The voice. Allen could hear it again, louder this time. It wormed its way through the darkness, coming from nowhere, so it seemed.

"Daryl? Guys? Is that you?" Allen spoke. He climbed on top of Autumn Crow's tomb and stuck his head through the gaping window. The goons were nowhere in sight. And while the voice could still be heard, it was fainter from out here. He brought his head back inside and the voice grew louder. It was definitely coming from somewhere inside. But where? It was a tiny crypt with nowhere to hide. No one could possibly be in here with him. Allen strained to make out the words. They sounded as if they were being spoken from the other side of a stone wall.

He looked at the tombs. *Could it be...?* He brought his ear to Autumn's first, listening for... what? A talking corpse? Growing up in Autumncrow, Allen truly believed in such things—believed them with all his heart. But he had to admit, the idea was a wild one. Still, he listened.

No... it wasn't coming from inside. Not inside this one,

at least. He crossed the crypt to Abraham Crow's tomb and pressed his ear to its smooth surface. Then he pulled away in shock.

No way... NO WAY!

It was! The voice was coming from underneath the lid. And not only that, but Allen could feel a draft of cold air emanating from the crack between the lid and the stone base. Whoever—whatever—was inside, they had a voice and they were yammering away.

Allen probably should have been afraid, but he wasn't. Instead, a sense of pure adventure possessed him. Before he could even consider his actions, he braced himself against the heavy stone lid and pushed with all his might, pushed until the lid finally gave. It slid to the edge, just enough for Allen to peek inside.

He didn't know what he was expecting to see. A living corpse, maybe? A ghost popping out of this dark, dark box in this dark, dark room just like in that old scary story? Whatever he was anticipating, it most definitely was not this.

Looking down into the tomb, he saw not the dead remains of Abraham Crow but a long stone staircase spiraling deep underground. Fire-lit jack-o'-lanterns sat to the sides of each and every step, grinning up at Allen, casting their long shadows on the walls. The voice, now distinct and clear, wafted up the depths of the passage, bringing with it a rank mustiness from years of moisture and decay.

Allen had found a real, honest-to-goodness secret passageway.

As if in a trance, he pushed the lid a little farther before thrusting his legs over the edge. He touched the first step with one foot, then the other. This was dangerous. He knew that, he really did. But he couldn't stop himself from descending the stairs. Isn't that what you did when you found a secret passageway? He had to see where this went. He just had to. And he needed to find out who was down there...

The voice was deep and raspy but had the energetic charisma of a gameshow host or radio DJ. "I thank you all again for joining me on this All Hallows' Eve, creeps! I will be right here into the dead of night, bringing you only the best in spine-tingling entertainment. Stay tuned because I have a doozy of a yarn coming your way... only on CRYP-TV!"

There was a brief pause, followed by the shuffling of feet and some plasticky clacking sounds that Allen recognized immediately as clattering VHS tapes. Yes, Allen knew what VHS tapes were. When he lived in Autumncrow, he and his friends would visit Undead Video, the retro-style videostore on Main Street, every Friday to rent a stack of horror films on VHS. The store owner, Rebekah, reminded them every single time that, "They don't make these anymore, dudes. These are very rare films, never even released on DVD. Protect them with your lives. Or else." She wasn't joking.

Underneath the kerfuffle of VHS sounds was the man's voice again, mumbling. "Where is it? Had it right here... Should have sat it out beforehand... Say it every time! Wonder if anyone is even watching... Probably out having a good time... Stuck here filming a show no one watches anymore... Ratings... Plummeting since the '90s... Should have cancelled the whole thing this year... Could be at the Mausoleum Ball... Nah, never been my thing—AH! Here it is!"

What is going on down there? Allen thought as he descended the stairs. He had never been so curious about anything in his entire life. He wondered when he was suddenly going to wake up in bed, discovering this was all an exciting dream.

If this is a dream, don't let me wake up.

Allen was halfway down the staircase now, passing pumpkin after pumpkin, wondering if the man downstairs had carved them all, wondering if he'd been the one to place the jack-o'-lantern outside the crypt. It dawned on Allen that the pumpkin hadn't been Daryl's prank after all.

The cassette tape could be heard sliding into a VHS player, followed by the clicking and whirring of the machine as it winded the tape through the track.

The archway at the bottom of the staircase stood doorless just a few steps away, the light inside flickering and dancing as if it, too, were some living being dwelling beneath the crypt. Careful not to make a sound, Allen took the final step and placed his feet on the dirt-covered floor. Then he crept toward the archway and peered through.

Allen's lips parted in awe.

The room was wide and cavernous. Large stone pillars were scattered throughout, bridging the gap between floor and ceiling. Spider webs clung to every corner. A casket sat propped open against a nearby wall, much like you'd see at a funeral viewing, except the man inside was long since dead, his bones holding what vaguely resembled flesh but mostly looked like burnt Hamburger Helper at the bottom of a skillet. For a moment, Allen thought the corpse had eyes that were wriggling about loosely inside its head, until he realized they weren't eyes at all but nests of squirming maggots.

Resisting the urge to gag, Allen looked away and surveyed the rest of the room. Structurally, it reminded him of Dracula's basement from the opening of the original Universal film. Except for the jack-o'-lanterns, that is.

They were everywhere. Carved faces of all kinds—some happy, some evil—stared at Allen from every tabletop, every open gap of the tome-infested bookcases lining the walls, every square inch of the floor. It was the most incredible sight Allen had ever seen, more incredible even than the pumpkin lighting ceremony during Autumncrow's Halloween Carnival.

Looking past the sea of pumpkins, Allen spotted a dated film camera erected in the center of the room, pointed directly at a little old man. Dressed in a ratted suit, he stood with his back to Allen, fooling around with the antenna of a TV box. The image on the television was slightly warped and fuzzy, but Allen could make out what seemed to be a skincare commercial. A strikingly beautiful woman with paper white skin and long black hair was seen holding a glass jar, showcasing it as if she were a model on *The Price is Right*.

"Skin not decaying fast enough?" she asked seductively. "No problem, babe. I've got your disgustingly perfect complexion covered with my brand-new skin mask, Madame Death's Peel-and-Scream. Just apply an even layer to your face, let it dry for ten to fifteen minutes, then peel it off nice and slow. If the first application doesn't rip the majority of your skin off your skull, bringing out those natural cheekbones, then you just hurry back to my store for a full refun—"

The image was overtaken by static. "Rotten thing!" the old man shouted, banging a fist on top of the TV set. "I won't upgrade to one of those plasmo television sets. You just can't make me!" He gave the set one final whack and the image was resurrected.

"You have my guarantee, babe," Madame Death concluded. "No bones about it." With a wink, she faded away into blackness.

"It's time, it's time!" the old man shouted, jumping away from the television. Tiptoeing around dozens of pumpkins, he rushed to stand in front of the camera. Now Allen could see his face in all its undead glory.

Allen wasn't as shocked as he probably should have been. In truth, he had seen so much oddity in the past few minutes that he hadn't expected the old man to be anything but a member of the living dead.

The zombie—for lack of a better word—had thin black hair combed over in attempt to hide a bit of brain-matter showing through the hole in his head. His skin was like dried leather, stretched so tightly over his skull that even with a closed mouth, his rotting teeth were exposed. Nose? Nonexistent. Eyes? Barely hanging in there. Facial bone structure? Madame Death would be proud.

Readjusting his black bowtie, the living dead man composed himself before pointing a brick-like remote control at the camera. He pressed a button. "Welcome back, creeps!" he said enthusiastically. "I am your host Crow Darkstorm coming at you dead from the catacombs of Kilgore Cemetery. I hope all of you in Autumncrow are having a Halloween to dismember. Next up on our CRYP-TV Halloween Marathon is a personal favorite of mine, one full of foggy graveyards sets and bad monster makeup. The living sure know how to make 'em, eh? Starring Bela Lugosi, I present to you... *The Return of the Vampire!"*

The man—this Crow Darkstorm—clicked another button on his remote and started the movie. Sighing, he let his excited nature slide. "I'm getting too old for this."

Allen watched as Darkstorm shuffled past the jack-o'-lanterns toward the camera. He had very little muscle mass remaining on his frame, but he attempted to lift the bulky contraption anyway. The camera didn't budge. Darkstorm's arm, on the other hand, snapped right off. "As I said before, too old!" He snatched the arm off the ground and reattached it with a loud *CLICK!*

Darkstorm stood back and eyed the camera. "Well, son," he said, "you can either hide there and watch me struggle all night or you can help an old guy out." Darkstorm turned his head and looked at Allen—directly at his face—and flashed an ugly smile.

For the first time in his life, Allen felt a weight in his stomach, a feeling most people refer to as fear.

"Uh... uh... I..." Allen stuttered.

"How did I know you were there? I may be dead, boy, but my senses are sharp. Come and help me. Please. I need the camera over there." Darkstorm motioned at a reading chair across the room, one surrounded with bookcases and piles of musty tomes. "Just be careful not to step on the pumpkins, please. I've been working on them nonstop for the past week. Coulda' used some help with those too."

Reluctantly, Allen stepped around the corner and into the room. He felt naked and totally petrified. What had he been thinking coming down here? What had he gotten himself into?

"Come now, don't be afraid," Darkstorm said. "Here, how about we introduce ourselves. Break the ice. My name is Crow Darkstorm, creator and host of CRYP-TV, lover of Halloween and the macabre, and founder of a little town called Autumncrow. And you are?"

Allen goggled at the dead man, at a complete loss for words. "F—Founder of Autumncrow?" he spoke finally.

"No, that's me," Crow said with a raspy chuckle that turned into a heaving cough. "Excuse me," he said, bending over and coughing up a cockroach. The bug hit the ground running.

Allen jumped out of the roach's way as it skitted past. "I—I mean... you founded Autumncrow?" he asked.

"That's what I said." Crow dabbed his nonexistent lips with a handkerchief. "Do you not have a name?"

"Allen. My name is Allen Morrisby."

"Well, Allen Morrisby, I am pleased to make your acquaintance. It's always nice to have company, especially on Halloween. You see, I used to live—well, I guess 'live' isn't the correct word... I used to *reside* in Autumncrow Cemetery until I decided to relocate here a year ago. It was such a busy place to spend the afterlife, all those ghouls coming to me with their needs night after night. It's been a lot quieter since I moved here. A little too quiet at times. But at least it gives me more time to put toward the show."

Allen didn't quite know what to do with all this information, so he said the first thing that came to his mind. "I just moved here from Autumncrow, too."

"Did you now?" Crow exclaimed. "Why, what a coincidence! Did you live in Autumncrow long?"

"My whole li—life," Allen said.

"My, my... and what did you think of my little town? Did it finally scare you away?"

"No! Not at all," Allen said. "I love Autumncrow. I never wanted to leave! It was my parents. They thought it was too dangerous for me. Too much weird stuff happens there. They were scared I'd disappear or something."

"Ah, I see," Crow said, stroking his chin thoughtfully. "How ironic. Well! Welcome to the neighborhood. Tell me, Allen Morrisby, how did you happen upon my crypt? Was it, let me guess... a dare?"

"How did you know?" Allen asked in disbelief.

"It's always a dare, isn't it? I imagine a group of small-minded teenagers dared you to spend All Hallows' alone in this crypt to see if you would survive until morning. Yes?"

"Well, kinda. They said I had to stay here until midnight. 12:30, I mean."

"Oddly specific time," Crow said.

"That's when all the scary stuff happens. Their words, not mine."

Crow laughed again and checked the large grandfather clock standing against a nearby wall. "And here it is, only eleven o'clock, and you're already having a conversation with a dead man. I'll bet you didn't expect the night to escalate so quickly, hmm?"

"Well," Allen began sheepishly, "honestly... no."

"Samhain is full of surprises," Crow said. "Now, no more dilly-dattle. I want to get my next shot set up so I have time to watch the film before I'm back on air."

Allen nodded, walking around the scattered pumpkins. He felt oddly comfortable in the presence of this ghoul. At first, he thought for sure he was going to be gutted and eaten, but now he was pleasantly surprised. He stepped up to the camera, getting a whiff of the foul-smelling dead man standing next to him, and lifted it from its stand.

"Thank you, thank you!" Crow said, gathering the tripod in his arms. "Over there, if you will. I'd like to wrap the rest of the night from my reading chair. Has a cozy feel, don't you think?"

Allen nodded, careful not to crush any jack-o'-lanterns beneath his feet, which Crow apologized for profusely. "I got a little carried away, it seems. Every night, I've been climbing out of my crypt and stealing pumpkins from a nearby pumpkin patch. Before I knew it, I had taken them all. I must have completely robbed that farmer of his livelihood."

So that's why Kilgore didn't sell pumpkins at any of the stores; they were all down here.

Crow sat the tripod in front of his dusty reading chair and Allen propped the camera on top. "That'll do, son. I appreciate the help."

"Yeah, you're welcome," Allen said. "Where did you get this camera anyway? And all the other equipment?"

"Garage sales, mostly," the dead man said.

Allen opened and closed his mouth, flabbergasted.

A grin spread across Crow Darkstorm's face. "Pardon. I'm just having a bit of fun." He stifled a childish giggle. "The camera was... donated, I guess you can say, by a man who was filming a documentary about Autumncrow back in the '80s. We encountered each other in the cemetery one night. He threw the camera down and took off running. Looked like he'd seen a ghost."

"You don't say?" Allen said.

"As for the televisions and such, I am ashamed to say I stole them from a RadioShack. Is that still a thing? Never mind. I don't condone theft but it's the only way a dead guy can get anything he wants these days."

"Your secret is safe with me," Allen assured him. "But why do you have a show, anyway?"

"The undead need entertainment too!" Darkstorm said. "And as you can probably tell, I have a passion for horror and spooky stories. My mother always told me, 'If you're passionate about something, you should share it with the world.' I did that in life and now I'm doing it in death. Also, if I didn't find something to do with my mind, I'd probably lose my time!" He cackled hysterically, making Allen leap backward.

Darkstorm choked back his laughter. "Didn't mean to startle you. Say! Since you have some time until the clock strikes twelve...thirty...how about you sit with me and watch *The Return of the Vampire?* It's an underrated film, in my opinion."

Allen couldn't help but smile. In a way, this reminded him of the movie nights he'd spent with his friends back home. "I guess that would be okay."

"Splendid! I have some chairs set up right over there. I'd like to introduce you to my live studio audience!"

To Allen's left, there were a few rows of old movie theater seats. Occupying most of the seats were skeletons, their bones clean and dry.

"Are they... like you?" Allen asked.

"Reanimated? Oh no, these guys are dead as doornails. No worries, son. You see, you need to be buried in

Autumncrow in order to come back from the dead. Something about the soil. In life, I knew as soon as I set foot on that territory that it was a special place, that it was where I wanted to found my town. My wife Autumn and I worked hard to build something incredible, and it came together like magic. A cozy little town nestled into the valley, one full of mysteries and intrigue. I loved the celebration of the fall harvest, see? Loved how it turned the world into a happy—albeit spooky—place. And there was just something about Autumncrow that enhanced that feeling. I think it had to do with those missing villagers. Ever hear that story?"

"Yeah, I learned about it in school," Allen said, taking the nearest seat. Crow sat down next to him, his joints cracking. "Those villagers settled there before the town was founded, but they suddenly vanished. No one knows what happened to them."

"That's right." Crow nodded. "I believe whatever whisked those people away left a curse in the dirt. That's all speculation, of course, but I used that curse to my advantage. I built a town that quickly became famous nationwide. I was a bit of a workaholic, my wife would say."

"Your wife, Autumn... she's the one buried in the tomb up there?" Allen pointed to the ceiling.

"Ah, yes. My Autumn. We met when we were young. She was wonderful. Unfortunately, she... passed away before we had much time together." Darkstorm stared down at his fingers and picked a sliver of skin from a rotten cuticle. "Toward the end, she began to change. Autumncrow does that to some people. When she died, I felt unsafe burying her in Autumncrow where she would rise from the grave, so I had her buried here instead."

"Why did you feel unsafe?" Allen asked. The idea of Autumn returning from the dead seemed to scare him.

"Oh, it's complicated," Crow said, waving him off. "I don't want to go into it. I'll just say that I wanted dearly to be buried with her. But if I had been, I wouldn't be around here to... look after things. My town needs me, and so does my wife's tomb. If she finds a way back, we're all in dang—" Crow froze.

Allen leaned forward, waiting for him to finish. *Danger.* Is that what he was going to say? That they were in danger if his wife was resurrected?

"Like I said," Darkstorm continued, "I don't want to talk about it. Bottom line, I had a tunnel built from here to my tomb in Autumncrow before I died. Expensive, yes, but worth every dollar. Now I can rest next to my wife *and* reap the afterlife benefits of my town, all while having an easy way back and forth. It's a win-win." Crow shrugged.

"Wow," Allen said. "But the tomb says your name is Abraham Crow, not Crow Darkstorm. What's up with that?"

"Crow Darkstorm sounds cooler," Crow said matter-of-factly.

With that, both Allen and Crow Darkstorm sat together and watched Bela Lugosi creep around on the TV set, looking no different than he did in *Dracula.*

"So, these kids that dared you to spend the night here," Crow began, "are they your friends?"

"No," Allen muttered. "All my friends are in Autumncrow. I don't have any here."

"Aww, that can't be true. Surely a nice young man such

as yourself has no problem making friends."

Allen shook his head and looked at his lap. "No. But it's okay. I don't want to be friends with anyone here. They're all mean and have no taste in cool things, and they all think I'm weird. In Autumncrow, no one thought I was weird, probably because everyone else was weird too. Here I'm just... alone."

Ever since he had moved to Kilgore, Allen felt nothing but anger toward everyone and everything. Now, he felt only sadness, a sick feeling nestled deep in his gut. *Homesick,* he thought. *I feel homesick.* He didn't mean for it to happen, but tears began to seep out of his eyes. He wiped at them, embarrassed, but that embarrassment only made him cry more. It wasn't like him to cry, but now he couldn't stop.

It was Crow Darkstorm's turn to stutter. "I... ummm... I, uh... hehe..." He patted Allen on the back awkwardly. "Uh—There, there. It's alright. Uh... here." He offered Allen his handkerchief, the one he'd wiped his mouth with earlier.

Allen laughed, wiping the tears away. "No thank you, Mr. Darkstorm. Really."

"Suit yourself." Darkstorm stuck the cloth back inside his suit pocket. "I understand the homesickness thing, Allen. I felt it myself when I first decided to move out here. All the people in this graveyard are too dead. But I have my wife." He sighed. "It gets better, kid."

"Yeah," Allen said, nodding. "That's what everyone says."

The grandfather clock began to chime midnight. Allen stood to his feet. "Well, Mr. Darkstorm, it was a pleasure meeting you, but I should get going. Those goons are going to be looking for me soon. Happy Halloween."

"Wait a moment now, Allen," Darkstorm said, standing to his feet. "I'm sorry to say this, but I can't honestly let you go."

"Huh?" Allen asked.

"You've seen a lot. A little too much."

Allen stared into Crow Darkstorm's goopy eyes, confused. Then the boy burst out laughing. "That's a good one, Mr. Darkstorm. Very good! I don't scare easy, but you got me. I'll see ya later, okay?"

"I am not pulling one on you, young man. I can't let you leave. You know... well, you know everything! And you see, a dead guy has to eat too. It's been a couple of months since any children have stumbled down here, but a Halloween feast? That's simply too good to pass up. You understand, yes?"

Allen felt that weight in his stomach again. It suddenly clicked in his mind. The missing kids... the skeletons sitting in those seats... Crow Darkstorm.

"You?" Allen said, shocked. "You were the one who took those kids? You... ate them?"

Darkstorm frowned. "Listen, Allen, I like you a lot. We have a bunch in common, you and I. But I'm really quite starved, if I'm being honest." Crow Darkstorm reached out a bony hand and grabbed Allen by the front of his jacket.

"Wait! Hold on!" Allen shouted. "You wait just one second. You don't want to eat me!"

"I don't. But I do at the same time," Darkstorm said. "It's a really confusing time, the afterlife. I'm sure you understand, being an adolescent and all."

"No! You really don't want to eat me. Seriously!" Allen yelled hysterically. "Why would you when you could have three very large, very dumb teenagers instead? It sounds like more than an even trade, if you ask me."

Darkstorm froze. "Yeah?"

"Yeah! Tell you what: you let me go and I won't tell a soul. I promise. I'll leave and pretend nothing ever happened. It'll be our secret," Allen pleaded.

Crow Darkstorm stared at Allen in doubt. "In that case, why don't I eat you and then wait for those three very large, very dumb teenagers to come looking for you? And then eat them too?"

Darkstorm had a good point. Allen thought for a moment and said, "I'm a good kid, Mr. Darkstorm. A very good kid. And those kids—the ones who dared me to stay here—they're not good kids. Wouldn't you rather rid the world of them instead of someone you claim to like? What would your wife think if you ate me? How would Autumn feel about that?"

This stumped Darkstorm. He paused, thinking long and hard, scratching at his brain through the hole in his head. "I knew I liked you for a reason. Okay, we have a deal. But only if you promise never to tell a soul."

"I won't. I promise," Allen swore, crossing his fingers behind his back.

"Fine," Darkstorm said. "Exit through the tunnel over there. It'll take you straight to Autumncrow Cemetery. Go. Go back to Autumncrow, find those friends of yours, and have the best Halloween of your life."

Crow Darkstorm attempted to give Allen a wink, but his eyelid just fell off and floated to the ground like a feather.

The two of them stared at it awkwardly for a beat.

"Thank you, Mr. Darkstorm. I won't forget you," Allen said, and meant it.

"Me either, kiddo. Don't be a stranger now. You can always come back and visit me."

"No offense, Mr. Darkstorm, but I don't think I will," said Allen.

"Fair enough," the dead man said. "Now go. Off with you! I need to prep for my meal."

Darkstorm walked excitedly to his kitchen area, getting out whatever supplies he thought would come in handy for taking down three very large, very dumb teenagers.

Allen, relieved yet disturbed, grabbed Darkstorm's camera from its perch and took off down the long dark tunnel leading to Autumncrow. He didn't know what he should do with the footage on this film—whether he should hand it over to the police or show it to his parents or post it on the internet—but as of right now, the camera was the last thing on his mind. Sure, the missing (eaten) kids were important, but at the end of this winding labyrinth was Autumncrow. His town. His home. The nightlong Halloween Carnival that was only just getting started.

Before he did anything with the camera footage, he would do exactly as Crow Darkstorm instructed; he would go back to Autumncrow, he would find those friends of his, and he would have the best Halloween of his life.

THERE ARE MONSTERS HERE

1

In my family, we each have our own monster.

They don't always show their ugly faces to us. Sometimes we'll have a day that is fine. Nice and quiet. Other days, one of us will see our monster peeking around a corner, its grin ghastly and wide, full of teeth.

At least, that's what my sister Miya always said about her monster—that it grinned. I never actually saw hers for myself, so I can't say for sure. That's the thing; nobody in my family can see anyone else's monster but their own. It's just the way it has always been.

I know Miya's must have been pretty bad though, if it was able to scare someone as stone hard as she. Like that time when I was six years old and Mother needed some things from the supermarket. She sent Miya and me to fetch them.

We weren't halfway down the cereal aisle before Miya stopped, her face growing pale. She pointed to the end of the aisle, mouth agape, eyes bulging. I didn't see anything except an Oreo cookie display.

"What's wrong?" I barely got the words out before Miya turned and darted out of the store, leaving me behind. Miya drove all the way home before remembering me, and even then, she was too afraid to come back.

It was Dad who came to pick me up. By then, I'd already done the rest of the shopping and was waiting in the parking lot with the paper bags. I should've waited inside because when I got home, I counted thirteen mosquito bites. I'd gotten more bites than that from playing outside after dark, but in my six-year-old mind, thirteen mosquito bites were unluckier than twenty-five mosquito bites or a hundred. Thinking back on it now, I'm pretty sure I was just unlucky to begin with.

Dad had never been as angry at Miya as he was then. I just felt bad for her. Felt bad that she thought she could run away from her monster. We all know there is no running. The presence was probably sitting in the passenger seat of Miya's car while she sped home that day, grinning at her the whole way.

The presence... Yeah, that's a good way to describe it, I guess.

That night at the supermarket wasn't what scared me the most though. What really got me was my mother's story of how she saw her monster for the first time. She never told it to me directly—she never spoke much to me at all, frankly—but I heard the story from my Aunt Jeanine.

It goes like this: One dark and stormy night when Mother was seven, she awoke with a dry throat. When she turned over in bed to grab her glass from the bedside table, the thing was there, crouching on the floor. Its arms hung limply by its sides so the backs of its hands rested on the floorboards. Its eyes glowed red.

When Mother gasped in fear, it hissed at her in reply and stepped a little closer, its knee making a strange *click* as it did. Mother covered her eyes and screamed for her parents, screamed for them all night long. But they didn't come. They were heavy sleepers.

Mother's monster never left her that night. It stayed until morning came. Even though her eyes were covered by her tiny hands, Mother knew it remained by her bed, peering at her through the darkness, its albino skin catching moonlight from the open window. She even heard it giggle a few times, as if her tears were jokes falling from her eyes.

As far as I know, Mother still can't sleep without a blindfold. Around the time she and Dad got divorced—I would have been seven—she even started using earplugs. Said she couldn't take the giggling any longer.

For about two years after the divorce, there were weekend visits with my dad. On Fridays, Dad would park his Jeep at the end of the driveway. I would dash out the front door, sprinting down the dirt road, my weekend clothes and playthings jostling about in my backpack. I would leap into Dad's arms and he would hold me tight, saying how much he missed me. Miya would then stumble past us, climb into the backseat, and slam the door shut. Miya hadn't always spoken in slamming doors, but she did at this point.

As the months wore on, so did my dad. I would run to greet him, but his hugs weren't as tight as they used to be. And he didn't say he missed me or that I was getting taller.

He'd just pat my back, buckle me in, glance at the house sitting a few acres off the road, and drive us to his apartment. Soon, he stopped coming altogether.

On the morning that Uncle Roland showed up at the front door of my childhood home, it was a sticky day like any summer in Louisiana. Though it was a thousand times muggier in Dad's old conservatory, it was still my favorite place to play.

In the two years since Dad left, the conservatory had become an untamed jungle. I'd explore every inch of it, tiptoeing through the green—a hunter chasing down his prey.

That day, I was crouching low on the jungle floor, tracking hoof prints, when I heard the doorbell chime. I ran from the conservatory and pulled open the front door. Uncle Roland's face drooped at the sight of me. This wasn't out of the ordinary. My uncle always looked sad.

"Hi," I said. "Mother's still sleeping. Want me to wake her up?"

"No, buddy," Uncle Roland said. "It's fine. I'll just sit and wait for her, okay?"

Without waiting for a reply, he squeezed past and made his way into the kitchen. A half empty bottle of wine stood upright on the dinner table. Roland sat down and took a swig straight from the bottle instead of asking for a glass. Mother would have wanted to finish the bottle off later that night, but I wasn't about to be rude to company. Instead of saying anything about the wine, I pulled a chair next to my uncle and plopped down.

"Uncle Roland? Where do monsters come from?"

He chuckled without smiling. "I dunno," he answered, and gulped down another mouthful of alcohol.

"They have to come from someplace, right?" I asked. "Do you ever wonder if they go other places when we can't see them?"

My uncle sighed, rubbed his eyes real hard and deep with his fingers. His eyeballs made squishy sounds when he did that. It made me want to gag. "They don't go anywhere," he said. "They're always here. You'll understand that when you're older."

"But what if they *do* go somewhere?" I pressed, climbing from my chair and sitting on the kitchen table. "They have to sleep just like anybody else. And if they can find us, we should be able to find them too. Like hunting a deer."

Uncle Roland narrowed his eyes and leaned back in his chair, crossing his arms over his broad chest. "What you going on about, boy?"

I shrugged my shoulders.

"Well..." He leaned forward. "If it helps at all, I guess if monsters go anywhere when we can't see them, they go home."

"Home?"

My uncle looked down at his callused fingers, folding them tightly in his lap. "Home is where the monsters are," he said. His voice was so low, I almost couldn't hear. "Monsters of men..."

His voice trailed off when Mother stumbled into the kitchen. She caught sight of Uncle Roland and stopped short.

"Oh!" She pulled her silk robe around her body and tied the tassel. I caught sight of several bruises on my mother's thighs. If my uncle didn't notice the bruises before she covered them, he certainly noticed the ones on her neck.

"I didn't hear you come in," she said, casting a nervous glance into the hall and up the stairs. "I overslept—"

"It's alright, Gracie," Uncle Roland said, standing. "Sorry to show up so early. I need to talk to you."

Mother froze for a moment. "Okay?"

My uncle looked down at me. "Why don't you give us a second, little man. Go hunt that deer you were telling me about." He winked.

I nodded and hopped off the table. My feet clomped over the wooden floorboards as I darted past my mother.

Before I got to the conservatory doors, curiosity prevented me from going any further. Uncle Roland didn't come about for casual visits. And usually when an adult tells a child to leave the room, that means they're about to reveal something important, right? I snuck back to the kitchen entryway, eager to hear the grown-up news. Pressing against the wall outside the kitchen, I listened.

"...jumped from the old bridge in town last night," I caught my uncle saying. "The doctors are giving him a few days. Grace, I'm sorry. I wanted to tell you before you or the kids found out from anyone else."

There was a long moment of silence. Then a tight intake of breath sounded from my mother. "He always was a coward," she said.

"Now Gracie..."

"Oh, hush up. You know it's true, Roland. The only brave thing that man ever did was marry into our family. But I should've known he wouldn't be able to handle it. All he's done since then is hide away in his little garden. Never once has he thought about me or his own kids. Even stopped picking them up for weekend visits. Did I tell you that? Stopped talking to them altogether. Never even returned my phone calls. And now he pulls this shit. Why am I surprised? Coward."

"Grace, come on now. You don't really mean that. You're upset."

Mother scoffed. "I'm not *upset!* I'm *glad!* I'm goddamn *GLAD!"* I heard a shatter and realized she had thrown the wine bottle across the kitchen. She did that a lot.

"Enough," Roland said calmly. But Mother was already hysterical.

"I'm not UPSET," she spat. "Are you kidding me?! I don't care about any of this! None of it! I don't care about *nothin'.*"

I peeked into the kitchen. Mother stood from her chair and waltzed to the cabinets, pulling down yet another bottle, bourbon this time. She was standing in broken glass while barefoot, but she didn't seem to notice.

Mother popped the cork off the bottle and drank. Wiping the excess from her mouth with her robe, she motioned to Roland with the bottle. "Except now he's left me to tell the kids about all this," she said. "How do you tell your kids their dad is about to die, huh?"

As if someone had jumped out and said, "BOO!" a jolt rocked through my body. I gasped. Chills swept over my skin. I began to tremble.

Daddy's going to die? Daddy's going to die?

"S'matter with you, kid?"

I spun at the sound of the voice. A man with shaggy orange hair and a gross beard stood at the bottom of the stairs. He wore no clothes other than a pair of red gym shorts. He rubbed sleep from his eyes with a fat hand. I had never seen this one before. But I still hated him. Hated him more than all the others, even.

Tears festered on my cheeks, burning my skin as my fingers balled into fists. A growl sounded in my throat. I ran at the big man and slammed my knuckles into his stupid, fat belly as hard as I could. He doubled over in pain and surprise. His face was low enough now that I could grab his scraggly beard and pull downward with all my weight. He didn't remain balanced for long. He fell over, right on top of me. I wriggled out from under his stupid, fat body.

"What are you doing?" I heard my mother scream. "What—? Stop it!"

"Ohhh," the fat man groaned. He must have face planted right into the floor because blood was gushing from his nose. "You broke my nose, you stupid runt. You broke my fucking no—*OH!*"

I kicked him one last time really good, right in his tiny, little gym shorts. Then I bolted down the hall.

"Scrawny bitch!" the man roared. "Get back here so's I can kill you!"

"Chris!" Mother yelled after me. "Christopher, baby, what happened?"

I ignored her and pushed through the doors of Dad's conservatory, slid over the corpses of plants littering the ground, and found a hiding place deep in my jungle.

I curled up and watered the plants with my eyes. It could have been minutes, it could have been hours—I'm not sure. But I do know I wasn't alone there. Through my tears and the foliage, I watched my monster's hooves as they paced back and forth, creating fresh prints in the dirt of my safe place.

2

Dad's monster had finally caught up to him. The police filed it as a failed suicide attempt. The doctors said the jump from the bridge had paralyzed him completely, leaving him unresponsive. But the bruise on his chest and the way his ribs seemed to curve inward showed that his monster was just perched on his chest, pinning him to the bed, staring him down until he took his final breath.

I think my dad really did jump from the bridge that night. Not as an attempt at suicide but as an attempt at escape. Just like Miya, he forgot running isn't an option.

I would tell the story of how I saw my monster for the first time, but I don't really remember it. As far as I know, I saw it the day I was born. It was in the eyes of my mother, in the freefall of my father, in the cold heart of my sister, in the emptiness of a family so scared, the very fabric under its feet was coming undone and letting every demon through.

No, this isn't the story of how I first saw my monster. This is the story of how I killed it.

3

I was twenty-four years old and I was depressed. Maybe if I'd been honest with myself, I would have caught it before it consumed too much of me. Maybe I would have asked for help.

Or maybe I *was* asking for help. Maybe I was screaming for it but had no one to hear me. After all, my sister was doing time for one too many DUIs, my mother had disappeared to her hometown in Ohio without a word, my dad was gone, and several other family members—Uncle Roland included—had suffered slow deaths at the hands of their monsters. Whether I'd been trying or not, there was no one to reach out to.

I guess there had been someone once, a couple of years ago. They ignited a spark of hope in my chest, a warm ember that made me think everything would be okay. Then something happened. I don't know what exactly, but something snapped. Our relationship was like a tree, slowly growing more and more beautiful from summer to autumn until finally wringing its skeletal hands of the leaves it once held close. I was one of those leaves, and I was falling to the ground with no one to catch me.

It happened to my parents, so why not me? Things like that never lasted, this much I knew.

Besides that, I couldn't find a steady job that would keep me. I bounced from apartment to apartment before ditching the struggle for the backseat of my car. It was comfortable enough, but I never really slept. I was too busy having staring contests with my monster. It liked to go from window to window, peeking in at me, its licorice eyes gleaming in the streetlight. I had a lot of time to study its features, the way its thick fur spiked if the night's breeze was cool, how immaculate it kept its black hooves, how narrow, its teeth.

I'd stare for so long that my body would fall asleep, while my mind remained alert. I was dead and conscious at the same time. I think that's why I no longer feared those dark eyes staring in at me. Waves of numbness eroded my every emotion, causing me to glaze over and forget how to be scared.

Not afraid anymore... Not afraid...

I marveled at the beast's long ribbed horns, awestruck at how they seemed to reach for the stars. Like if they reached far enough, they would snap free from the head that bound them and pierce the sky. Those horns, so intricate and lonely. I wanted to break them off and set them free.

That's what weaved the idea in my mind.

I hadn't been afraid of my monster for a long time. I wasn't afraid of anything. What had I to lose other than a piece of shit car, a drool-stained pillow, and a worn paperback copy of *The Hobbit?* My life? I wasn't truly alive. And the part of me that remained—the one making my heart pulse—wanted something better than this life. I was no different than one of those horns, reaching for an escape. Maybe if I gave them that escape, I'd get one of my own.

Freedom. The word crept into my mind, producing a shiver that raised every hair on my arms and legs. I bolted upright in the backseat, coming face to face with the beast. It heaved a breath from its dog-like snout, steaming the window that separated us. I stared into those black eyes as a plan formed in my head.

"Home is where the monsters are..."

4

I pulled down the long driveway of my childhood home. The white colonial had stood abandoned since my mother left five years ago. I'd hit the road two years prior to that, just shy of my eighteenth birthday. This was my first time back in almost a decade.

Illuminated by the harsh glow of my headlights, the abode appeared the same as it always had—glorious despite its blemishes. Beautifully flawed. And yet, just as cold and unwelcoming as ever.

My car bumped along the drive, hitting every pothole and loose stone, until I came to a stop. I killed the engine. Silence held me in her arms. There wasn't a sound as I opened my car door, no crunching of gravel as my feet met the ground. Even the forest bordering the right side of the property was quiet, though it still reeked like a fish tank gone unkempt. You never get used to the smell of a bog.

I started up the porch steps, expecting each one to groan under my weight. They didn't. Just more silence to prolong an echo of tension. By all laws of nature, the night shouldn't have been this stagnant. But the night isn't a fool either. It knew what awaited me through that door and it was biting its nails, anxious to see the events unfold.

I reached the front door and pushed it open. There was no creaking of hinges to announce my arrival. Just the cold light of the full moon washing over the floorboards, tinting them a bluish hue. At first, I was surprised that the door wasn't locked and bolted, but the house must have known I was coming.

A sudden howl came from the forest, snapping the silence in two like a spine hitting concrete. My body tensed in the doorway as I listened. More yelps and hollers sounded from the trees. Growls, roars, maniacal laughter.

An animal would not dare break the silence at a moment like this. No, these weren't the sounds of nocturnal animals—these were the cheers of monsters. Hundreds. I could almost see them in my mind, waltzing together in circles deep in the forest, parading over leaf and stone, celebrating the lives they had taken.

Never once did I think it was possible to hear monsters other than mine, but I did now. And I hated them. Hated them more than my own, even. I slammed the door, putting an end to the wild rumpus of wild things.

"Oh, please don't go—we'll eat you up—we love you so!"

I found myself standing in the foyer, stairs off to the right beside the living room archway, entry to the kitchen on the left. Straight ahead, past the stairway, was a hallway leading to the conservatory. I could see the doors at the very end. They heaved in and out, as if they were breathing. The wood groaned and cracked. The sound of a hibernating bear met my ears. Deep intakes of breath. In, out. Calm, but forewarning. *Do not wake me, boy.*

We had so much in common—my monster slept while the others danced. The perfect time to end it all.

I took a step down the hall, just one, before a voice stopped me. "Christopher? Is that you?"

The stench of alcohol floated from the kitchen. I swallowed.

"Is it you, son?" the voice continued in slurred words. "Have you come to kill me? Would you really kill your own mother?"

I closed my eyes, releasing a stuttered breath. I didn't look into the kitchen. I couldn't and *wouldn't*.

"You're not my mother," I spoke just above a whisper.

It's your monster... Your monster...

A chuckle. The sound of feet stumbling over floorboards, coming toward me. "You're just as ignorant as your daddy. Think it and make it so."

"No, that was you," I shouted before I could stop myself. "You always did that!"

Don't argue, Chris. You know that makes it worse. Just keep going.

Grimacing at my lack of control, I took a step down the hall toward the breathing doors, then another.

"Sure, just walk away from Mommy," the thing that sounded like Mother continued. I heard the slosh of liquid in a bottle. A gulp. "You all walked away from me. Left me alone in this godawful house. Oh, how many nights I awoke at the edge of that forest, wanting so badly to venture inside and never come out. All because of you. But no. Not me, I didn't do that. No sir! I'm *strong*. I moved on..."

I kept walking. Drunken footsteps fell in sync with my own.

"...I'm *strong* and you're *not*. You're weak, lying in your car all the time, pouting over people who never truly loved you."

The voice was getting deeper, sounding less and less like my mother, drawing nearer to my ear.

"You're weak, Christopher." *Deeper.* "You make it easy for me." *Nearer.* "Easy for me to tear you apart from the inside out."

Not Mother, I repeated in my mind. *Not afraid anymore.*

The voice said nothing more. The footsteps retreated to the kitchen.

A memory of my mother flashed in my head, a memory of her opening the liquor cabinet and biting the wooden door in rage when she found it empty.

Not afraid anymore... Not afraid...

I drew closer to the breathing doors, close enough to touch the splintered wood with my fingertips. I twisted the doorknobs and pushed. A strong gust of fowl smelling wind—as strong as any hurricane—pushed back. I resisted, forcing with all my strength until I was able to squeeze between the doors and stumble into conservatory. The doors slammed shut behind me, and the hurricane winds ceased as if they had never existed to begin with. All was silent again except for deep intakes of breath echoing off the walls.

I was back in my jungle. It hadn't changed much except that it was far more overgrown than the last time I'd seen it. However, being the old friend that it was, I knew the terrain well. Like Bilbo Baggins entering Smaug's cave, I padded through the thick foliage, unsure which way to go. Stopping, I listened.

No. There was no way to know. The breathing sounds came from everywhere at once, toying with my sense of direction. So, I sniffed the air instead, catching the scent of damp fur. And beneath my feet, hoof prints.

Now I have you.

The prints were as large as my fist, if not bigger. They led over a path crowded on both sides by thick lavender bushes. I pushed through them, remembering how the plant irritated my skin as a young boy. I itched my forearm and continued following the trail.

The breathing was indeed growing louder. Louder, that is, until I reached a dead end. It was then that the sound cut off, and so did the hoof prints. All that stood before me was a tree that reminded me of a small weeping willow, its long branches meeting the ground, creating a fort to hide under.

I remembered this. This was the place I had gone when I found out about my father, where I had cried so many tears.

That's when I heard the sobs of a young boy. There, right in front of me, under that sanctuary of leaves. My heart rate quickened. I pushed away the green. A little boy was curled up on the jungle floor, hands covering his face as he cried. His knees were covered in dirt, his clothes soiled with grass stains.

And suddenly, he wasn't a boy anymore. He was a beast covered in black fur and horn. His breaths were uneven, tail swooshing from side to side, fingers creating deep trenches in the dirt as he dreamed the blackest of dreams.

I felt a gasp erupt in my throat, one that didn't reach my lips. I swallowed and knelt low on trembling legs.

Not afraid...

I pulled a knife from my pocket and unfolded it. A quick thrust to the head was all it would take. I just needed to be careful and as silent as possible, even if it meant suffocating from holding my breath for so long. I leaned forward, bracing myself like a bridge over the monster's body. Its hot breath warmed my wrist. I imagined it waking and clamping its teeth around my arm, ripping it from its socket.

Closing my eyes for a moment, I focused on calming my nerves. It was impossible.

Just one quick thrust and it would be done. *Kill it. Kill it like it has killed you all these years...*

I drew closer and held the blade to the base of its neck. Now that I was this close, I noticed the fur was covered in a sticky black substance resembling tar. The scent was vile, like a rotting corpse with clammy hands reaching for my face. I pushed my nose into my shoulder to avoid gagging.

Don't breathe, I reminded myself. *End it already.*

But when I turned my gaze back to the beast's face, its black eyes were wide open, staring straight up at me.

Oh, God, no! Oh, God...

My monster snapped its huge jaws upward with a snarl, narrowly missing my face. I tumbled back, watching in panic as it scrambled to its hands and knees, then to its feet. It towered seven feet above me, peering down with bared teeth.

"N—No," I whispered. Fear overtook my senses. There was no longer a sheet of glass separating us. I stared directly into the eyes of the monster. What did I see? Not happiness, not love, not guilt, but a simple vacancy of all things good. Everything around me was gone, a bright-red blur. All that was once there and could have been was there no more. I was alone with the beast and it was approaching.

I managed to achieve my footing and turned to run, but the slashing of claws across my back sent me flying through the air. I landed in the lavender bushes. My back was ablaze with pain, blood soaking the lavender beneath me. I clenched my teeth and willed the pain to fade, prayed for it to end.

My monster crept forward, crouching low so only its horns and eyes peeked above the underbrush—a shark's fin cutting water. This sight was terrifying enough that I forgot all about my pain and hopped to my feet, running through the foliage toward the clearing ahead. Dad's workbench was there, next to a rusty spiral staircase leading to the upper balcony.

A roar sounded from behind. Running, I glanced over my shoulder, watched as my monster leapt into the air, its powerful legs launching it several feet and bringing it to a halt at my heels. It stretched out its fingers, ensnaring me around the neck.

I gasped, twisting my body and prying at its claws with my hands. Its grip only tightened. I was lifted off the ground. The other hand wrapped around my legs, raising my body higher and higher until I was over the monster's head.

For a moment, I thought it would drop me onto its horns, impaling me with the very things I wanted to set free. Instead, I was thrown across the conservatory into a clearing. I landed on a solid surface, heard something *crash* under my weight. I sat up with a groan. Dad's old workbench was in a splintery heap beneath me.

My monster stood in the center of the clearing, chest rising and falling with each angry heave. *Got you...* those black eyes said. *I've got you...*

I rolled off the wreckage that used to be my dad's bench and attempted to push myself off the floor. My energy, however, was diminished, both from the fall and from the blood rushing out of my back. Breathing into the dirt, I lifted my eyes to keep my sights on the monster. I was shocked to find that it was no longer with me.

My dad was.

He didn't give me any notice, just looked around at the overgrown state of his conservatory. Frowning, he lifted a pair of hedge clippers off the ground. He made a few hopeful clips at a shrub. Then his shoulders slumped, the clippers leaving his fingertips and clanging to the ground.

He raised his head enough for me to see his eyes. They were the saddest eyes I'd ever seen.

A small childlike whimper left my lips. "D—Daddy?"

No, my heart said. *You know it's not.*

Dad's lips moved, but it took a moment for the words to reach my ears. He was like an actor in a dubbed foreign film. "I wish I could've taken this place with me," he said. "It's the only thing I would have chosen if I'd had a choice."

"Dad..." I repeated. It was all I could say.

He shushed me. "No, Christopher, don't say anything. I really can't stand to hear your voice right now." The words were soft spoken but sharp. "I wouldn't have chosen you, son. I was done with you sucking the life from me. You were weak and needed someone strong. I couldn't be that person for you. You were too much a burden."

Don't listen. It's lying, trying to break you down. Your dad isn't here. He's dead.

"Had it not been for you and your sister, I believe your mother and I would still be together. My jungle would look beautiful..."

I shook my head, pushing my hands through my hair. The murmurings of my father still found their way into my ears, even after I blocked them out with my hands. I focused on the work boots in front of me, trying to convince myself it was not my dad's feet that wore them.

Suddenly, Dad's words ended, and his boots were no longer there. Instead, I saw another pair of familiar shoes. I knew right away who they belonged to.

My blood turned to ice. "No..." I whispered.

Don't look!

I looked.

My eyes shot up and saw a face I never thought I'd see again, never wanted to see again. It was a face I'd loved, a love truer than the love for my dad or Miya or my mother... Oh, God. I realized I still loved them all, even after everything.

This face, the way it made my heart race even now, showed me I still loved it as well. But it hurt like hell itself.

Still not real. You're not afraid...

But I *was* afraid. I was trembling uncontrollably. Maybe I always had been trembling, in my sleep or whenever my mind would fade, whenever I was unaware and couldn't stop myself from being scared to death. Maybe I only stopped feeling because I'd trained myself not to. Maybe I'd always been erupting inside, waiting for this moment to pour out.

My eyes flooded with tears. "Please," I begged, my voice too small. "Don't do this..."

The lips moved and spoke, carrying my words away. "Hey."

I closed my eyes tight and fell forward, sobbing into the dirt. "I'm b-begging you. I-I c-can't..."

"You need to relax, Chris. You're too dramatic."

I couldn't breathe. It felt like my lungs were seizing up, like my heart was falling to pieces.

"That's called heartbreak, Chris. I thought you were too numb to feel any of that stuff. So much for not being afraid anymore. Seems like you're worse off than ever. And you look like shit, too."

"Please, stop," I begged through the sobs. "I can't do this. It's t-too muh-much."

"It's too much to feel, you mean." The words were

harsh. Indifferent. "You were never really good with feelings. It's not unnatural to feel things, you know." A pause. "Hey! I have an idea... how's this feel? I never loved you."

I grabbed my chest as another wave of pain twisted my heart—twisted my whole body—and tossed me onto my back, like there was a wild animal in my chest pulling me in every direction at once. Laughter echoed all around me, shrill laughter with a deep monstrous base beneath it.

"S-stop," I begged. "Please. Don't do this to me..."

The laughter ceased, and those eyes looked into mine with mock sympathy. "You've been all down in the dumps since I left. And now I'm back and you're having a fucking panic attack. Even after all this time, you *still* don't know what you want. You're pathetic."

"Why?" The word broke through my sobs all on its own. Just saying it seemed to ease my panic, just a little.

"Hmm?"

I wiped tears from my face and, as calmly as possible, asked the question that had haunted me for years. No matter how bad the answer would be, at least I'd have some closure. That's what I hoped for, anyway. "Why did you leave? Y-you said you never would, and then you did."

As if the moon outside was being swallowed up completely by darkness, the conservatory grew dimmer with my every word. "Why did you go?"

The figure in front of me wasn't so much a person anymore as it was a faint shadow. Silence stole every sound. My heart began to pound in panic yet again, but I couldn't hear it. Just felt it.

"Why?" I repeated. "Tell me."

The dark figure answered in the deep, gravelly tone only a monster could have. "You started mourning me before I even left."

It's your monster, Chris. You're losing sight of why you came here. It's lying to you.

No, it wasn't lying. Not this time. This was the first shred of truth my monster had spoken all night.

Very few good things ever happened to me in life, but whenever I had any luck at all, any positive influence whatsoever, I pushed it away out of fear. I thought it was too good to be true. I had chances to escape my past, but I wasted them. That was the truth.

"You're right," I said, lifting my chin, feeling the sadness fade and acceptance take its place. "You're right. And I'm sorry."

The darkness in the conservatory lifted slightly and my monster was back. It didn't seem to like my response. With a growl, it got down on all fours and darted my way, stopping just inches from my face. Its snout opened in a roar, showing dozens of teeth placed haphazardly on its jaw. Spittle covered my cheeks.

I fell backward and—remembering something I could use—darted to the side, narrowly missing the swipe of my monster's claws.

I hit the dirt and the monster followed, landing on top of me, crushing my body, jaws snapping at my face. With all the strength I could muster, I held the beast around the neck to keep its teeth from my throat. I reached with the other hand, reached, reached until my palm met with my dad's hedge clippers. Then I swung them around.

I felt the impact as the blades plunged into my monster's

trapezius muscle, felt it between my own neck and shoulder. I screamed in pain, and at the same time, my monster let loose a roar more ferocious than any other. Warm blood spilled over me, filling my mouth and flooding my eyes. The weight of my monster let up and I sat forward, wiping the blood from my face. I peered down at my hands, surprised for a moment. I don't know what color I expected, but I certainly didn't anticipate so much red; it was too human.

The beast stumbled around the clearing, back slamming into the spiral staircase, hands pulling at the clippers lodged between its neck and shoulder. With each tug, I felt it too—the pain shot up my neck and down my spine. I placed a hand there and looked at my fingertips. Blood covered them, but not my own blood. Only the monster's.

Then I knew; whatever pain my monster felt, I would feel it too. We were one and the same. But if I killed the monster, did that mean I, too, would die? Maybe. But that didn't matter to me. I was ready to feel all its pain.

The beast's attention was occupied, so it didn't notice when I stood to my feet and limped toward it.

Kill it. Kill it.

I moved as quickly as I could, grabbing the clippers and yanking down with all my weight. They slid out surprisingly smooth, but my monster and I howled. Blood spurted from its wound. Pain clouded my vision.

My monster took a blind swipe at me, but I dodged, just barely. Stepping forward, I shoved the clippers into the thing's gut. We cried out together, but quieter this time, with less energy.

The beast collapsed to its knees, swaying in front of me.

I propped a hand on the nearby staircase for support. That's when I saw the handsaw dangling from a hook to my left.

I remembered the horns.

I realized what I had to do.

Snatching the saw from the hook, I neared my monster. It was on its stomach now, heaving as it bled out. I dropped to my knees, straddling the beast, and wrapped an arm around its thick neck. I pulled with all my strength, hearing the monster groan. But it didn't put up a fight; it had already lost too much blood.

I raised the saw to the right horn. And I began.

Back and forth, side to side, deeper and deeper, metal to bone. My monster moaned and whimpered like a deer after being struck by headlights. A deep ache pressed at the top of my skull, so deep it pulsed in my heels. It was miserable, but I continued like a madman in his lair. I reveled in the pain, pain I should have felt for so many years but never faced.

Until now. It was time.

I finished with the first horn, pulling it free and setting it in the puddle of blood beside me before starting on the next. My monster slackened in my arms, the life draining from its body more and more until the saw snapped through the last bit of bone. At this, the monster's head hit the floor with a crack, leaving the horn in my hand. My monster didn't move.

I picked up the other horn, turning them in my hands, staring at them. Then I dropped the horns onto the back of the beast, covered my face with my blood-soaked hands, and started to scream.

5

I walked down the porch steps to my car, gravel crunching underfoot. I no longer heard the monsters in the woods, but I could feel them watching from the trees, hanging their heads in mourning.

I wasn't mourning.

I had set my own shadow on fire and watched it burn. I was a lost boy no longer. I was free.

I opened my car door and sat inside, turning the ignition. My headlights lit the face of my childhood home like a candle. I thought, only for a second, of striking it ablaze before leaving. But I decided not to. It was a house where bad things had happened, to me and to others, but it was only a house now. And while a part of me died in there tonight, a better part lived on.

I smiled—something I hadn't done in ages—and a tear fell onto my cheek. Putting my car into gear, I turned and headed down the driveway. I could almost see a younger version of myself outside the window, running next to my car. I could almost see Daddy standing by his Jeep at the end of the drive, arms outstretched. And was that Mother and Miya I saw too? Standing next to him? Laughing?

I thought maybe I should go visit Miya, track down my mother, start over with my ex. But no. It was what it was. Something better was awaiting me, something good.

As I pulled out of the driveway and onto the road, I remembered my uncle Roland. *"Monsters of men..."* he had said. That man had been right about a lot of things, but he had been wrong about that. There are no monsters of men.

We are men of monsters.

Acknowledgements

A book is like a jack-o'-lantern. There are a lot of things that need to happen before you can set it on your front porch for the neighborhood to see. There's the planting of the seed, the watering, the picking off the vine, the planning, the carving, and (of course) the lighting of the candle.

I first have to thank my mom for planting the seed. Had it not been for those hours spent at the library and the countless bedtime stories, I wouldn't be writing these words right now. *It Didn't Frighten Me* then and it doesn't frighten me now! I also need to thank my dad for encouraging my writing every day and never once thinking I was incapable of reaching this point. To my siblings, thank you for embracing my weirdness and for putting up with all my 'gotcha' scares. I was only practicing!

Then there's the people who watered the seed. Thank you, Ms. Clark. You came to my rescue when I needed you most and pushed me to take writing seriously, even at a young age. I'd also like to thank Mrs. Landes, Mrs. Russell, Rachel Hock and the rest of the Writer's for Him group, my Bookmobile family, the Night Worms crew, and my YouTube creeps for supporting me for nearly a decade (and counting!).

To the people who visited Autumncrow when I was just beginning to map it out... thank you Emily Wright and Jonathan Tripp, as well as my patrons—Ahmad, Aspasia-Dina Gordon, Basy Nightshade, Billy Norfleet, Brad Clarke, Chris Baumgartner, EarthsGeomancer, John Anthony, Kevin DeLisle, LittleRetroBoy6, Ryan Burrows, Sebastian Larsson, Señor Scary, and Stanford M. Brown. I am truly blessed to have your support.

Thanks to the people who helped carve the jack-o'-lantern: J. David Osborne for making these stories look so much better, Elizabeth Easter and Edward Lorn for your help with *There Are Monsters Here,* my name brother Cameron Roubique for creating the most killer cover art I have ever seen (and I've seen a lot of good covers), Christopher Rondina for doing such a great job on the cover layout, Adam Cesare for answering all my questions, and Jeff Van Meter for your input and for being the best friend I could possibly ask for. And to God (for everything).

Lastly (but most certainly not least), I would like to thank you, the reader, for following me in and lighting the candle.

About the Author

Cameron Chaney was raised in a small Ohio town you've never heard of. He spent his childhood roaming his family's six-acre yard, devouring one book after another, and dreaming up monsters and ghouls. He can now be found working on the Bookmobile for his local library, typing away in his office, or geeking out over books and horror on his YouTube show *Library Macabre*.

Visit Cameron on Twitter (@bookmovieguy), Instagram (@bookmovieguy), Facebook (@LibraryMacabreBooks), and Goodreads. Don't feed him after midnight...

Printed in Great Britain
by Amazon